T0114638

Shackles of Freedom

Malthouse African Fiction

Shackles of Freedom

A novel
By

Onyeka Ike

Malthouse Press Limited

Lagos, Benin, Ibadan, Jos, Port-Harcourt, Zaria

© Onyeka Ike 2016
First Published 2016
ISBN 978-978-51932-9-9

Malthouse Press Limited
43 Onitana Street, Off Stadium Hotel Road,
Surulere, Lagos, Lagos State
E-mail: malthouse_press@yahoo.com
malthouselagos@gmail.com
Tel: +234 (0)802 600 3203

Dedication

For Nenwe; the noble land of my birth, and for Gani.

Gathering Clouds

Chapter One

The cloud was dark, heavy and roaring. It was impregnated with the first major rain of the year which had reached the peak of its gestation period and was, therefore, tired of dwelling any longer in the accommodating womb of the cloud. So the pregnant cloud was in pangs of labour; about to give birth to a heavy rain in the month of May. The weather was a bit cold as a strong moist wind blew across the Sahara, rolling the thick cloud southwards as if to strip the heavens completely naked.

Major Shigaro sat calmly at the veranda of the officers' mess sipping steadily but uneasily a big bottle of Guinness Stout. A full plate of steaming goat pepper-soup was also facing him on a well-carpentered, low rectangular mahogany table. When he finished eating and drinking, he held his two muscular arms across his massive chest, leaned on the brown leather sofa and stared menacingly at the rolling cloud as though he had a score to settle with it. But he had no quarrel with the cloud; no grievances with the firmaments; no disgust for the weather. It was rather with the oligarch in khaki uniform and the affairs of a tottering nation.

A military mafia spearheaded by a dark-goggled General was holding the country hostage. The General, perhaps, considered himself a special breed who was born to rule perpetually. He was in the clique of ambitious soldiers who severally conspired to abort democracy in Nigeria and substituted it with treachery, dictatorship and agonizing tyranny. The average citizen wept for hard time as the

General oppressed, intimidated and managed the country like a personal estate. He believed that he had the knife and the yam, and would cut out a piece for whoever he wanted to give.

Before now, a few persons had approached Shigaro and offered to assist him financially to oust the General whose dictatorial regime had inflicted untold injury to the citizenry. Despite several protests and sanctions to return the country to a civilian democratic leadership, she had remained in the hands of the mafia who had plundered and raped her in turns, and were ready to do even more. It had been over a year the offers started coming to Shigaro from within and outside the nation. Those who dangled the carrot at his face were people who had either personally observed his chemistry or were informed of it. So they knew that he was capable of springing a surprise if only he could make up his mind to do so.

Shigaro knew the General too well. He knew that he was a tiger who shouldn't be touched carelessly at the tail; otherwise he would chew his prey to pulp as it had been done to many officers. So, accepting to attempt to topple him was like deciding to take an irreversible journey in the footpath of either life or death. If he succeeded, he would live. But if he failed, he was sure that he would be slowly roasted alive over a high temperature furnace. He was sure that he would go the way of unsuccessful rebels.

A thousand thoughts besieged his mind; a million questions inundated him. Would he bell the cat? Would it be successful? What if it failed? Would he pick the dangerous side of the coin? Then he would pay the supreme price; a very costly price - his precious life and that of his fellow conspirators. Is Nigeria worth it? Should he remain indifferent and watch helplessly like others? The price for its failure was too scary. Would his three children ever forgive him if he chose to abandon them fatherless when they needed him most? Where would the judgment of history place him? He knew that he had no democratic inclinations; no patience for dialogue and consultations, just like the tyrant he was contemplating to, probably, oust. Would his only brother, Dr. Konja, a physician, who had often spoken about his brother in the army, find a place in his heart to forgive him if he failed and died as a rebel; a coup plotter? Shigaro's thoughts were endless. And as he rose to depart, he asked his orderly to go and tell Captain Kokoma to see him in his flat in the evening.

Shigaro was departing when he saw a newspaper vendor passing by. He stood and called him. When the boy hurriedly got to him and greeted, "Gudivini, sah!" he simply ignored the greeting and began to scan through the cover pages of the newspapers and magazines.

There were *The Punch, The News, Vanguard, Sunday Times, Daily Times, Newswatch, Concord, Champions, The Source* and *BBC Focus on Africa. Newswatch* and *BBC Focus on Africa* immediately caught his attention. He paid for them, collected them and swung into motion. When he got into his flat and banged the iron door after him, he pulled out his expertly polished black boots and began to read through some of the major stories that caught his interest initially.

He first picked *Newswatch* which had three major stories on the cover page. The cover story read: **BASU WEEPS FOR HER SONS.** It was a detailed and well-written story which thoroughly reflected the pulse of the Basu people, the masses of the country and indeed the international community concerning the gruesome murder of Koolo and eight of his kinsmen. It also chronicled several other low and high profile politically motivated homicides in the land. The story was a pathetic one; the type that could make one to shed tears while reading it; the type that could make one lose a peaceful sleep for several nights. The title of the next story on the cover page read: **CRACKDOWN ON THE OPPOSITION:**

9

SECURITY OPERATIVES IN PURSUIT OF NADECO CHIEFTAINS. The other story was rather a question which had remained in the mouths of many Nigerians for several years: WHO KILLED BOLA OLUWA? It was a million dollar question.

There was Bola Oluwa's photograph beside the big question mark. He looked handsome, robust, clean and erudite, and was smiling as though he was celebrating his birthday; as though he was standing before his birthday cake with a knife ready to cut it; as though he was surrounded by his wife and children cheering him up; as though he was still alive - hale and hearty. His well carved moustache was appealing - the type that could sway any beautiful lady. His jet-black padded hair rhymed with his suit and bold tie. It was an epitome of corporate dressing. The picture in the inside page was entirely different. It was a gory figure of the same man; mutilated and shattered with a letter bomb in his own sitting room.

Shigaro did not spend much time in reading through the entire cover stories as he impatiently dropped it and picked *BBC Focus on Africa*. The cover story read: TAYLOR RECRUITS MORE CHILD-SOLDIERS. The next title read: **African Nations at the Brink of Total Disaster**. It was a brightly-coloured, well-packaged magazine. On the same cover page were certain images of war, hunger, *kwashiorkored children*; images of unkempt and disillusioned people; images of refugee camps and disaster infested areas; images of tribal wars and unbridled dictatorship. Everything the magazine reflected on Africa was ugly. As if Africa was a continent handed over to Satan and his cohorts; as if other nations of the world never fought wars - their wars; as if they never had a period of depression and hunger; as if there was nothing good at all in Africa; as if it was only a continent of evils; as if everything in it was all about kwashiorkor, wars, disasters, diseases and dictatorship; as if Hitler was not a German. It was as if Mandela was not a citizen of the African continent; as if Emeagwali did not design the fastest computer in the world; as if corruption was a native of Africa; as if it built its permanent headquarters in Nigeria; as if every Nigerian was a fraudster - the reason they are scanned to the pants at the airports; as if the true blood of a Kenyan man does not flow through the veins of Obama.

The time was 6.30p.m. Shigaro was smoking marijuana in his sitting room when Captain Kokoma of the Armoured Corps entered. He had knocked at the door for almost three minutes before Shigaro could realize that someone was seeking for his attention. He was consumed in a habit which he so much relished. Shigaro became an addicted smoker since he clocked sixteen. But it was hard for someone he did not tell to know about it because he usually appeared healthy and tough. He had the kind of brain that effectively cushioned the immediate influences of marijuana. He rarely took weaker sticks like St. Moritz or Benson & Hedges because he believed that such smokes would not sufficiently charge him. He also enjoyed his drinks - mainly hot drinks and concentrated liquor.

Shigaro's upbringing and early life was as hard as iron and as difficult as climbing Mount Kilimanjaro. But he had a natural iron-cast determination to achieve whatever purpose he set before himself. It was indeed his belief that the only obstacle that could deter a man from realizing his objective was his willpower to succeed. So when he decided on any cause, he burned his boat completely till he saw the end of it.

He carried himself with an air of rarity which was not altogether baseless because even as a Major, he had become a near phenomenon in military circles, especially among officers of his rank and below. He had achieved a lot for himself as an officer and for the nation whose territorial integrity he swore to defend several years ago. Shigaro was firm, averagely brilliant, courageous and daring - a non-yielding leftist radical infantry officer who was also plagued with ambitions; the love for naked power and the irrepressible desire for the limelight. His well-cherished career philosophy was to yield to nothing. But he could, at times, sink into the ocean of depression if the thought of his unpleasant childhood overwhelmed him. He was a gold medallist at their passing out parade as officer cadets of the Nigerian Defence Academy. And when he was sent to Liberia and later to Congo on peace keeping missions, he distinguished himself and made the country proud as he returned with awards of excellence and gallantry. But while his course mates were now lieutenant colonels and colonels, he had remained a major for over seven years because he had no godfather to push his file to that effect.

As Captain Kokoma stiffened and saluted smartly, he waved him to an opposite sofa in the sitting room; with an unusual smile of friendliness, puffing out thick clouds of smoke through his nostrils. The captain had worked directly under him for nearly a year at the Brigade Headquarters. Kokoma had shown a high sense of commitment to his duties and unflinching loyalty to Shigaro as his immediate boss. He knew that Kokoma believed in him and had, in his natural loyal manner, been working with him wholeheartedly at the fuel directorate of the brigade. Dipping his hand into a nearby gleaming metal drawer, Shigaro pulled out a bottle of twenty-two year old British rum, dark as charcoal, and placed it on a low rectangular glass table facing him and his guest who had picked *BBC Focus on Africa* which he was quietly poring over. Kokoma was an avid reader. Two tiny Italian glass cups also emerged from the same drawer and landed on the same table.

Shigaro returned from England with the much valued drink when he attended a special course on Infantry Tactics at the prestigious Royal Military Academy - the British highbrow officer-factory in Sandhurst. He shook the rum and opened it with fascinating skill and expertise; he pulled the tight cork gradually and intermittently until it blew open, releasing a thick cloud of Carbon IV Oxide. He half-filled his glass and then that of Kokoma. They simultaneously lifted them and clicked to long life and success. Shigaro took his first gulp of the liquor and grimaced as it sent an intensely burning sensation down his throat. It was like a burning flame. Kokoma followed suit, still holding the BBC *Focus on Africa* magazine in his left hand. He grimaced repeatedly before he dropped his glass. After some awkward moment of silence, Kokoma spoke:

"Why can't this people, for once, see anything good in Africa? This is the type of report we always see in every edition of this magazine."

Shigaro was silent for a little while before he said:

"Captain, you are from a black race in a continent of Third World countries. Can anything good come out of Nazareth? That is the way they see us."

"But that's not totally true. Admittedly, we have our numerous problems, man-made problems, but that does not mean that they should always see us in a bad light, as if those who are seen as powerful and prosperous today did not crawl before they started walking and, perhaps, running. Every nation and continent has its own share of earthly troubles."

"Captain, you should have gone to the seminary. You could have been a better preacher than a soldier," Shigaro grinned.

"Sir, I am being frank. The Western media are hardly fair to us. It is mainly the ugly occurrences in Africa that they readily show to the world. Such is not edifying; not good at all."

"They are entitled to their opinions. I don't care what they see or say or show to the world about us. I have no time for such sentiments. Anyway, let's leave that matter for now." At this, Shigaro lifted his glass to take a gulp. Then there was some silence.

Kokoma gave his attention to reading more stories from the magazine.

"When are you guys going to write the Captain-to-Major promotion examination?" Shigaro asked.

"In August, sir."

"Where?"

"In Maiduguri."

"Ah! Maiduguri. Ours was at 82 Division. Enugu was such a fine place - beautiful landscapes from Ogbete to Ogui. I spent an extra day at Nike Lake Resort before returning to base. It was a fantastic experience."

"Enugu is a nice place," Kokoma responded. "I was there for five years as a student of Federal Government College."

"Really?"

"Yes, sir."

"So, how are you preparing for your forth-coming exams?" queried Shigaro.

"I'm doing the best I can, sir."

"Do you have the relevant materials?"

"Yes, sir."

Shigaro grinned. Kokoma reciprocated with a benevolent smile of one engaged in an informal discussion with a respected senior.

"You have three more months to prepare."

"Yes, sir."

"How many children do you have now?"

" Four; three boys and a girl. My wife first gave birth to triplets who all happened to be males. Then she gave birth to a baby girl two years ago. Presently, she is pregnant."

"You are a strong man," Shigaro said as he grinned. Then he inquired: "How did you cope with rearing triplets with your meagre salary, or did you get any political appointment or some juicy contracts?" Shigaro asked in a lighter mood.

"I was an ADC to a military Governor in an oil-rich state. His Excellency was of great help; so it wasn't really a big challenge to us then. We had more than enough."

"No wonder," Shigaro responded. He took another gulp of the liquor. "When will your wife be due for delivery again?"

"In six months' time, sir."

"Then you would have returned from Maiduguri."

"Yes, sir."

"Men, you are lucky."

"Thank you, sir."

"When did you get married?"

"Five years ago. Just a year after I left the Academy."

"Where is your wife from?"

"She is a Kalabari woman." "Is she one of us; a soldier?"

"Not really, sir. She is a full time house wife for now. But she is a graduate of Law from the University of Port Harcourt."

"A lawyer?"

"Yes, sir."

"How do you cope with having a lawyer as a wife; those people can be troublesome and argumentative? They have never stopped talking about fundamental human rights and equality, even at the home front."

Kokoma smiled. "It depends on the individual, sir. Some of them are quite good and can make good homes," he then said.

"You are very lucky. You have a smooth-sailing career, an educated wife and a good home too. No woman has ever lived under the same roof with me as a wife for more than two years. They say that I'm too difficult and intolerant; that I'm too soldierly. But that is rubbish - absolute balderdash. Women are all a nagging specie. They create a lot of problems for themselves with their tongues, yet they cannot withstand the consequences of their rattling. They are weaker vessels. My three children are from three different women who are no more with me. But I have three mistresses who visit whenever I need any of them. Women are the same everywhere," Shigaro stamped with finality and grinned again.

"It may be true, sir."

"Yes, it is true," Shigaro concluded firmly, nodding simultaneously.

There was a little pause as both men lifted their glasses to drink. As soon as they dropped their glasses, Shigaro pressed further with his questions:

"How many more children would you like to have?"

"I'll be okay with the five, sir. In fact, we would have gone for family planning a year ago, but my wife insisted on having one more baby before we do that."

"How are you sure that Oliver will not want some more since it appears you always succumb to her whims and caprices?"

Kokoma took another gulp and grimaced. Shigaro's hand hadn't left the glass cup either.

"Not always, sir. But a man needs to submit to some of the views of his wife if the home must be peaceful."

"No. It shouldn't be so," Shigaro retorted and grimaced.

"A man who hands himself over to what we call women in the name of anything is not fully qualified to be called a man, especially if he's a soldier. He should rather be called a biological mistake. And I think there are many men like that. They're not supposed to bear that name 'men'. One is not a man just because he dangles a pair of testicles between his thighs. Soldiers ought to be soldiers. Yes, that is true. When a cobra procreates, what you have is a multiplication of venom. A cobra that is weak and not deadly is a

16

bastard, counterfeit, misbegotten and certainly not worthy of the name," Shigaro added. He poured some more drink into his cup, took a gulp and grimaced again. Then he slightly scratched his thoroughly scraped, gleaming head.

Kokoma was alarmed. He paused for a while because he could not yet decipher where Shigaro was heading to, along the line of some of his utterances. But he had started to perceive that he wasn't, after all, invited just to have a leisurely evening together with his immediate boss. Not for an ordinary discussion. But the handwriting on the wall was yet to appear legible, he reasoned. The worry soon showed on his face.

Shigaro quickly noticed that Kokoma looked a bit uncomfortable. So he decided to digress, to bring him back to a lighter mood.

"What was your next assignment after the ADC stuff?"

"Soon after His Excellency left office, he recommended me to General Shilanga to be his orderly. It was from General Shilanga's office that I was later redeployed to this place."

"General Shilanga?"

"Yes, sir."

"The oil-magnate?"

"Yes, sir," Kokoma said as an exuberant smile ran through his face. Shigaro grinned.

"That means you must have a lot of money by now. Your bank account must be fat, very fat. Isn't it? You must have purchased some choice properties by now. Or perhaps you have changed your money into dollars and made a reasonable savings into a Swiss Bank as some of our Big Ogas are doing. They do it for safety reasons. Ah! Only God knows how much of Nigeria's oil money that has been stashed away in Switzerland, Holland, London and Germany and several other places. Sadly, much of it would not even be utilized by those who stashed them there until they die. Well, let's leave that for now. That is by the way. It is one of those things. You are indeed very lucky to have served as an orderly to such an Iroko in the military. Aren't you?" Shigaro asked and grinned.

"He is a good man," Kokoma responded.

"Good indeed," Shigaro retorted good naturedly with a tinge of irony Kokoma didn't fail to notice.

Kokoma was calm. He kept quiet for a while and flipped through the magazine pages.

"How did you see the pulling out parade of General Degema yesterday?" Shigaro asked.

"Perfect; well-organized; well attended. It was a good ceremony befitting for a man of General Degema's status. He really rendered meritorious services to our dear nation," Kokoma answered.

"Don't you think that it was rather untimely to retire Degema at this period? A number of his course mates are still in the army? Since he served our nation meritoriously as you said, he ought not to have been retired abruptly."

"Yes, it is true. But you know that the Commander-in-Chief is no more comfortable with General Degema's popularity in the military. So he was sent packing, even though he ought to have spent at least five more years with us in the service," Kokoma answered.

Shigaro was joyfully relieved that Kokoma had somehow, indicted the C-in-C for wrongdoing; that he had blamed him for General Degema's untimely retirement. But Shigaro did not betray his joy. His face remained expressionless. Yet it was obvious that the captain merely spoke his mind, spoke the truth, without really attaching any feeling of indictment to it. It was clear that he had no personal grudges against the C-in-C, even for his hand in Degema's untimely retirement. He was not a man given to grievances and vendetta, but could merely express his mind wherever and whenever it was convenient, without any intention to hurt anybody. He was a professionally sound and simple-hearted officer.

Shigaro overlooked these and latched on to Kokoma's last statement to unveil part of his true feelings, the very reason he had invited him to his sitting room for the first time; the purpose for the unusual smile of friendliness and his generosity of expensive drink.

"That is the issue. It was a clear case of victimization- untimely retirement. Once he perceives you as a threat or a potential threat he either kicks you out as he did to Degema or ropes you up in a phantom coup."

Kokoma grimaced, almost unconsciously. Now, it wasn't because he took a gulp of the liquor but because of the mention of the word "coup." It was a word he was never comfortable with anytime he heard it. So he became more conscious at this point.

He knew Shigaro as a serious minded and determined officer who would not just mention such a dangerous word in such a manner and circumstance without having something in mind. And judging from the way the unusual discussion had been going, Kokoma was now fully convinced that something serious was in the offing. Something was at stake.

There was dead silence, except for the clicking of their glasses on the table as they gulped their drinks. Kokoma showed no sign of volunteering any more comments because he reasoned that Shigaro should have told him precisely what he called him for before now. Moreover, he had just thrown a bombshell by mentioning, in a suspicious manner, a word which level-headed officers like him dreaded—coup. He was usually uncomfortable with the word, not because he lacked the requisite courage to be part of it, but because of the unpredictable consequences it could have over a long period of time on the nation, whether it succeeded or failed. He was a good student and analyst of History, having bagged a B.A. degree in the same discipline.

Kokoma focused wholly on the *BBC Focus on Africa*, reading the magazine as if his next promotion exams depended on it. He read from line to line and refused to betray any emotions. Shigaro observed this. He was not bothered because he understood the game he was into. He knew that it was never an easy one. The whole enterprise was intended to capture Kokoma's heart firmly and then channel it to the actualization of the difficult cause he had already chosen. He knew how useful Kokoma would be to him if only he could endorse the cause. He reasoned that he seriously needed the backing of a highly committed and loyal armour officer like the captain because he would be of great help in rolling out the tanks on the D-day. After a period of silence that seemed like eternity to Kokoma, Shigaro spoke again, his voice now calm and sober:

"How did you see the execution of that man and eight of his disciples by hanging in Port-Harcourt last year?"

"You mean Koolo, the renowned author and environmentalist?"

"Precisely."

"It was sad. I believe that it ought to have been done differently. The option of hanging should not have been considered at all. At worst, put them behind bars..."

"But the C-in-C thought otherwise. It was a gruesome execution. Wasn't it?" Shigaro asked.

"It was...sir" Kokoma nodded.

"I also thought that it ought to have been done differently from what we saw. After all, their agitation was for the survival and collective wellbeing of their long neglected people. That was also Captain Dako's main point of agitation, and why he remained defiant and remorseless before General Chukwu's tribunal; that was what he said prompted him to join the Orkar group; that the land of his birth which produced the nation's wealth had nothing to show for it; that their people were suffering a lot despite the enormous resources nature had showered on them. Wasn't it?"

"Yes, it was," Kokoma nodded again.

"They ought to have been given a listening ear," Shigaro said, "at least, consider some of their demands—save their environment from complete degradation, give education and jobs to their youths, and provide solid infrastructural development to the area. That would have been better than spilling blood in such a wicked manner. I really felt bad when I saw the man's septuagenarian mother on the screen pleading for clemency. Yet nobody listened to her until her son and the others were taken to the gallows."

"I heard that he predicted that Shell would be brought to book some day in a court of justice for their alleged collaboration," Kokoma responded.

"So I also heard. But that type of justice is rare. It comes once in a life time," said Shigaro.

"Any nation which continues to waste such men, such gifts of nature on the altar of strife and politicking is in a great jeopardy. I was an ardent viewer of his popular TV Soap Opera, Basi and Company. I have also read a number of his newspaper articles and books. Well, justice might still come as the man predicted; only that no one knows when and how..."

"That is the issue!" Shigaro interrupted.

He observed that the last issue he raised in the discussion had stimulated Kokoma's interest a great deal. The captain now appeared a little more vibrant and relaxed. Shigaro was encouraged by that reaction but did not make it noticeable.

"That is the issue," Shigaro repeated after a little silence. Then he asked Kokoma:

21

"Did you hear him refer to Bubar's regime as *kabukabu* presidency, meaning that it was wobbling and unreliable?"

"Yes, I did. I read it in one of his writings. It was a funny neologism, sir."

"There's nothing funny about that. I did not really like the way that man was cruelly handled by the C-in-C. I believe that it ought to have been done differently since his principles and methods did not actually threaten our corporate existence as a nation. It was a mere agitation for a fair treatment. And the issue of the death of the *vultures* could not be substantiated. The man had maintained that he had no hand in their deaths. We could have avoided further waste of lives. I was not surprised that Mandela called the C-in-C a mad man on account of that incident. Yet it did not bother him," Shigaro said.

"And he replied that Mandela had spent too long a time in prison to come to terms with current realities. That was how he dismissed Mandela's comments. You see, Bubar was wise enough not to have touched that man in that manner all through his administration. He only used security operatives to harass him; to respond to the protest marches he organized. But the C-in-C had a different approach," Kokoma responded.

"Captain, don't be ridiculous. Bubar is an evil genius, and he had acknowledged so by himself. That he used the harassment approach does not make him entirely different from the C-in-C. I consider both of them birds of a feather."

There was silence again. While Kokoma glued his eyes on the magazine again, Shigaro simply kept mute and waited patiently for his response. He needed, at least, another good response from the captain before he could delve into the grave matter for which he had actually invited him to his house. Kokoma tore the silence which lasted for about four minutes:

22

"It was an unfortunate incident. I also did not like it. No American or European country could have wasted such a supposedly national asset. That is one of the reasons they are very far ahead of us. They have noble minds; they value and preserve what they have; they pursue excellence; they believe in themselves and in their nations; they work for their common good, believing in their collective efforts to building great nations. And they are proud of it. An average American, for instance, first of all thinks of the collective well-being of his country before personal considerations. That's how I think it ought to be if good legacies must be bequeathed to posterity. But here, the reverse is the case. That's our major problem as a people. An average Nigerian, first of all thinks of the good of his stomach; his family; then his tribe before he remembers the country, if at all he does. He mainly thinks of what he will grab for his stomach and for his ethnic group which he erroneously believes should always dominate the others; should always be in control. That is our problem; no genuine consideration for other people. So the country becomes a mere geographical expression that exists only on paper and not in the hearts of the people. No one really knows when that trend will stop; when we will begin to reason properly." By this time, he was going through the *Newswatch* magazine.

Shigaro held his peace for a while, staring into space. Then he cleared his throat once and started to talk:

"Captain, you are a patriotic soldier. I admire your brilliant ideas. But remember that America also had its times of troubles before they came to where they are today. I know that with people like you on board, there could be changes."

Kokoma did not understand what he really meant by saying "...with people like you on board..." but he did not want to ask him, to avoid sounding disrespectful to his senior. Instead, he said, "Yes, I had earlier said that every nation and continent has its own

23

problems. I am only pointing at the things that have kept us where we are today. We need to overcome them as a people so that we can move forward."

Then there was silence again, a longer silence. Shigaro gulped the remaining drink in his glass and silently stared into space, reasoning whether it was indeed fully ripe to dig into the grave issue or to beat about the bush a little further. Kokoma busied himself with the magazine and did not seem to be in a hurry to go. Even if he was, he would be the last person to tell such to a senior officer, one he respected a lot for that matter. He was a man of matchless loyalty, patience and courtesy. Shigaro knew it.

Shigaro cleared his throat once again and fired what he considered as the first major shot.

"Captain, what do you think of the situation in the country now?" he inquired, fixing his eyes directly on Kokoma's face. Kokoma paused for a while as he stared at the glass cup he had equally emptied some minutes earlier. Then he spoke:

"Not too good, sir. People seem to be suffering...."

"People are suffering daily. Suffering amidst plenty resources. That is the issue," said Shigaro with much enthusiasm. Then he continued: "Can there be no solution? Can there be no peace? Don't we deserve it? Can there be no way out of our myriad of problems? Why should one man hold the entire nation to ransom like this?"

Kokoma was alarmed. He knew that the hour had come for the hand writing on the wall to register fully. But he remained calm even though his inward being was already agitating. Shigaro perceived it. There was silence again, a brief long silence. Shigaro shattered it, fixing his eyes on Kokoma's countenance once again.

"Captain, the C-in-C should go. He must go. This oil does not belong to him alone. Has he not eaten enough? He should go so that others would take their turns. We are aware that Okigbo panel report also indicted him for his collaboration in siphoning and mismanaging over twelve billion dollars of our oil money realised during the Gulf War. That's a whooping sum of money. I think he has been in the saddle for too long. Now, he is arranging to transmutate into a civilian president. For what? I do not buy that idea. Nigeria is not his family property. No! We will not allow him to continue to manipulate everybody. Is he the only officer trained in Aldershot? If he does not want to step aside and quit peacefully, he will go in pieces. I can assure him of that. Yes, his time is up and something must be done about it. We must not all be feminine. Of what use is a he-goat without testicles? Of what value is a tiger without teeth and claws? Something must be done soon."

Kokoma shivered inwardly as Shigaro rained down those words with impunity. It was becoming more visible that his heartbeat had increased a little. Kokoma battled to contain himself, reasoning that it was unsoldierly to give himself away too cheap by showcasing his fear. And when Shigaro added, "... done soon" with an air of finality and firmness, as if he did not know the man he was talking about; as if he could just chase him out of the throne like a chicken, with a wave of his hand; as if it was an easy task, Kokoma became more shattered, and the battle to contain himself intensified. He was speechless. He was downcast; he didn't expect it that way. It was as if the day of his death had just been fixed and announced to him.

It seemed to him that he had just been informed of a plot he must be a party to; without seeking his consent. How soon was soon? He knew he could not ask his immediate boss such a question. Shigaro had spoken like someone who had reposed enormous confidence in him; like someone who never contemplated any possible disappointment from Kokoma. Indeed, he had. Hot blood rushed into Kokoma's head and seemed to have covered his two eyes. Was he daydreaming? Was it real? Would he go to report the matter? Would he let him down? What would be the end of the plot?

Dead silence fell on both men. The period seemed like a lifetime for them both. It was a total, deafening silence. No glass clicked on the table anymore; no hand turned the pages of magazines. The word "soon" began to form a heavy, moulded block in Kokoma's head; in his imagination. It began to hit his head as though an experienced carpenter was hitting him with a massive Monday hammer. He had said "...Soon...Soon...Soon." Could he say anything to the contrary? He had not been given the opportunity to, probably, say so. Kokoma stared at the opposite wall with disillusion. It was cream-painted with Shigaro's larger than life photograph neatly tucked on it. It was the picture Shigaro took a day after the eagles landed on his shoulders. It was good-looking, neat and spectacular. There were also other pictures taken at different periods of his military career, starting from his days at the Academy as a cadet officer.

While Kokoma stared endlessly, Shigaro patiently waited for his reactions. The dice had been cast before him. And he seemed not to be given alternatives to decide for himself. The iron-cast major had sounded double sure that Kokoma would not disappoint him; that he expected him to stand with him on the cause without any equivocation. Had he been given options, Kokoma would probably have made a choice; his own choice. Kokoma remained calm and neither talked nor betrayed much emotion. His heart though was beginning to pound a little faster than before. He battled harder to contain it, to make it unnoticeable to Shigaro who seemed very relaxed and unperturbed. Shigaro rather brought out another brand of liquor, poured into his glass and began to gulp it with a spectacular ambience. For a while, no verbal response was volunteered by Kokoma because he had not yet found his voice.

Shigaro decided to follow him up with a question. He tore the looming silence:

"Captain, do you think that we can do something in the present circumstances? Do you believe that we are capable of doing anything at all? Don't you see that we can spring a successful surprise and change things for good? Rawlings and Castro did it in their times and succeeded. We have no other option than to succeed. We can make it; we only need to believe in the cause and be courageous as good soldiers we are. How I wish there is a better way of doing it than the route we already know. It is the same everywhere. The road to political power is smeared and strewn with blood. That is the only option every soldier in uniform has in the game of power. The C-in- C has become a masquerade that must be unmasked. You should be on our side, our arrangements are intact. We can make it."

Kokoma maintained his calm, but Shigaro was not bothered. Nevertheless, he could now see clearly that Kokoma's heart was pounding and how the officer tried hard to conceal it. Kokoma's mind raced endlessly. He pondered over some of Shigaro's sharp comments: "...we can spring a successful surprise and change things for good ... Rawlings and Castro did it in their times and succeeded...." He remembered that Major Nzeogwu, Colonel Dimka and Major Orkar were not lucky in their cases. Yet Shigaro didn't mention them. He only told him those who succeeded; just one side of the coin. Kokoma's heart told him that the method Shigaro opted for in his quest to capture political power was becoming unfashionable in modern times; a time when people all over the world were clamouring for democracy, equity, justice and good governance. Yet he could not resist it. Was he even safe if he said no? Was it his fate? His destiny? Would he be the traitor? Had he the courage to resist it? Did he know the extent Shigaro had gone in the plot? Kokoma's mind continued in thoughts. Then he seemed to have recollected himself a little. Kokoma found his voice and asked soberly:

"Should we touch the tiger by the tail? I am averse to bloody changes. Can it be bloodless?"

"We will not only touch the tail of the tiger but also seize it by its jugular," Shigaro affirmed.

"How do you intend to contain some members of the political class who are already on rampage, clamouring for democracy?"

"That is not an issue," Shigaro dismissed with a wave of his hand. Then he continued: "We know them; we understand them. Some of them are mere political and ideological prostitutes. Their real motive in most of those agitations you see on the pages of newspapers and elsewhere is far, very far from being altruistic. As soon as we succeed and are able to hold forth for even a week, they will surely cross-carpet. It will happen. They will come to beg us to be appointed ministers and special advisers. They will lobby us to become members of the Provisional Ruling Council and lick our feet to be given juicy contracts. Mark my words because it will surely happen. And as long as Ghana-must-go continues to change hands, they will continue to twist their tongues to say whatever we ask them to say, even more. Many Nigerian politicians have no conscience and they can do anything to get what they want—the idols of their hearts. It is only a negligible few that are different, and you can be sure that their number is too small to withstand us. Of course, you know that we can comfortably handle them. The majority will certainly fall in line with us in order to get what to eat. So we know them. Which coup succeeds here without seeing people beating drums and dancing in some streets? They only make noise when they have nothing to eat; when you give them nothing to chop. Then they will trouble you. I understand them very well. If you can give the noisy ones some plum appointments in the government or as board members with good Ghana-must-go, they keep quiet and even clap for you with all their strength. I agree with them that a hungry man is an angry man. They are always ready to change their language; to sing new songs so long as you know how to handle them. So that is not something to worry about."

"What do you think of the Shola factor? That Lagos-based radical lawyer and pro-democracy crusader can be a thorn in the flesh of soldiers in power. He could be very troublesome and unyielding; he could attempt to mobilise the entire country against us."

"Captain, Shola is one vibrant and committed agitator whose courage I admire a lot, but I do not fear him, not even in this matter. I know I can handle him perfectly. So leave his matter for me. We will cross that bridge when we get there."

"How do you intend to handle the Western power bloc and the obvious pressure they will mount on you to return the country to a democratic rule? Their sanctions? You know that they have a lot of interests in Nigeria and have been clamouring for a democratic order. Do you think that they will tolerate another military government as a replacement to the C-in-C's, sir?"

"Captain, America and Britain can only make suggestions to us and not compel us to do anything, period. They can't force anything on us. They are sovereign; we are sovereign, period. They determine what happens in their lands, we determine what happens here, period. Have they really succeeded in short-changing the C-in-C? That is the issue."

"I am with you, sir," Kokoma submitted, his voice almost trembling halfway into the statement.

It was a very weighty statement; as heavy as a block of lead. Kokoma understood all the implications. He knew that he had endorsed either life or death, that he had chosen a difficult cause, which can either raise or drown him in a matter of time. He knew that his well-founded and cherished career had been put on a hard line, where history would either reckon him as a hero or a rebel. Whichever way, he had already appended his signature by giving his word of support for it. And there was no turning back. The rest, he reasoned, would be left for fate and the judgment of history.

Shigaro stood up to have a warm handshake with him and proceeded to glue his body on his in a hug. Kokoma saluted him again and opted to leave. Shigaro perceived that the captain was shattered and really needed to put himself together. Kokoma's legs seemed even heavier as he took one step after another. It was as if the weight of his body had suddenly become too heavy for his legs to carry; as though his muscles had lost their functions. He had never contemplated to be part of such a plot in his life or career. Now that the idea had come around him or seemed to be imposed on him, he could not resist it. He seemed incapacitated to do so, only saw himself giving his consent, his unwilling consent. And he knew that he would still not change it; he was already part of it and, therefore, would either live or perish with it.

Kokoma was a level-headed career officer who loved his job and was contented with his salary and other benefits his job could peacefully provide for him and his beloved family. It was primarily due to his professional capability and exemplary loyalty that Shigaro insisted on applying for his services, having closely studied him for quite some time. So he knew that he would not let him down if only he could succeed in extracting his promise as he had just done. He was not an ambitious man.

Unlike Shigaro who was naturally a high-wire adventurist—a professional risk taker, Kokoma always looked forward to having a more fulfilling career, and a peaceful retirement as a General, with full benefits and honour. So taking the type of risk he had just endorsed had never been part of his agenda in life. Before now, he had the exciting prospect of establishing a decent fish pond and poultry farm after retirement. There he would stay to cuddle his children, grandchildren and great-grandchildren, he reasoned. He was fond of telling his wife that their happiest years were yet to come. He was referring to life after active military service. Now that he had endorsed a dangerous and uncertain script, such a dream could be a mere mirage. The failure of it could shatter everything for him, including his dear life. No one was ever sure of his fate until what would be came to be. It was a route which does not lead the same travellers to the same destination. One takes it and reaps fortune and glory, another takes it and is cut short and dumped in the dustbin of public odium, ridicule and contempt—the same route.

"There's no turning back," Kokoma muttered to himself in utmost determination. Then the man and soldier in him returned. He would certainly not let Shigaro and the cause down. He would not spill the beans; he was already a party to it and would either live or die with it. He hoped he would live and not die. He would keep it a top secret until he was summoned for action, an action that could determine the fate of a nation—an oppressed nation, a nation in the firm grip of wicked forces.

Shigaro saw him off to his car, an elegant ash-coloured Nissan Blue Bird. Shigaro returned to his sitting room and sat down quietly to think. Rising up almost immediately, he proceeded to his room, loosened his belt and pulled off his khaki trousers and his white singlet, pulled a thick brown towel round his waist and went to shower. After a hasty bath, he wore grey knickers, returned to the sitting room and sat down calmly as he did before. He engaged his mind again in a calculated race of thoughts.

Kokoma returned to his own apartment and could not help being worried as he thought over the concluded talk. This was despite a resolution not to allow it to bother him. It was a difficult evening for him because his mind was constantly on it. That same night, sleep became a labour for Kokoma. It was a burden he couldn't lift as he kept toing and froing on his bed until dawn. Neither he nor Shigaro lived in the barracks with their family members. They had made them settle down in other relaxed and comfortable locations where their children attended schools. While Kokoma's wife nursed their children, Shigaro employed the services of a twenty-two year old foster mother to take care of his three children. Her name was Margret. She had been abandoned at birth and did not know her parents. Hardly a weekend passed when Kokoma was within the country and would not travel to see his family. As for Shigaro, he never ceased to send money across for the upkeep of his children and for the payment of their foster mother. He would visit them once in a blue moon when he considered it necessary or when his feelings rose to touch Margret's big boobs and to see her beautiful figure.

As Shigaro sat calmly in his sitting room, he continued to calculate his strategies: considering a number of possibilities and obstacles, and thinking of other professionally sound and committed officers he would apply for their services. As his eyes raced steadily and boldly from one corner of the sitting room to another, he suddenly remembered his unpleasant beginning in life which usually irritated him, making him unhappy and sometimes, depressed.

It was the events of several years ago which he often wished could be completely erased from the album of his mind but to no avail. If Shigaro was given the privilege to make a choice, he would not have chosen to come to the world through the type of parents that gave birth to him. Even as a child, he closely watched a man's inhumanity to a woman he did not really love, but whom he reluctantly accepted to pay her bride price and bring home as a wife. When Zamuna—Shigaro's mother—saw that she had been turned into a miserable punching bag in what was supposed to be her happy matrimonial home, she opted to be a knife and not a wife. Nothing else had ever haunted Shigaro's imagination more than this rancorous, hostile, difficult and unpleasant home which he saw as his.

Chapter Two

Shigaro was the product of a broken, battered home. It could be aptly said that it was in his family that he first saw war and diligently studied infantry manoeuvres. It was there that he first saw action, though not as a soldier but as a tender boy. And he kept the matter to his heart.

Zamuna, his mother, was by nature a good woman. But a wrong vehicle of relationship and marriage conveyed her to a wrong hand that turned her into a tigress. So, a mutual anarchy existed between husband and wife. As Shigaro grew up, he became more convinced that it was a biological mistake and injustice for him to have been conceived through his parents. He felt that providence was not considerate enough to have sent him to such an unpleasant couple. If at all he was given a split second consultation, he would have vehemently rejected coming to the world through their loins. But like a tree, he had no choice on where he was planted. Shigaro saw himself being planted on a rugged and seemingly infertile terrain.

Whenever Genje hit his wife with the fist and muscle of a man, Shigaro would stare at him with hatred in his eyes, as if he wanted him to die instantly and leave his mother alone. He disliked seeing his own mother crying like a baby, with no one to come to her rescue. Genje was mercilessly brutal. The only thing that could deter him from hitting Zamuna hard was his physical tiredness. Then he could use his tongue which was quite venomous. Genje had an uncontrollably fiery temper; as fiery as a rattle-snake. But he could partly shield these traits if his manly affection grew towards a free woman as it did to Zamuna several years back, or if he needed to work for someone to make some money to take care of himself.

If eyes could kill, Genje would have been slain by the regular menacing stare of Shigaro who happened to be one of the biological products of his numerous nocturnal sexual escapades. Genje greatly loved what was in skirts, and could turn into a real amorous he-goat if his passions overwhelmed him as it did, sometimes. Shigaro hated him with passion even as a little boy and as he grew older, saw his father as an embodiment of irresponsibility. Genje drank and philandered boundlessly. But for Zamuna's courage, eloquence and vividness of expression, Genje would have denied her and her three months old pregnancy as he had done to many others. So it was with much reluctance that he accepted responsibility and paid Zamuna's bride price. Shigaro always felt like a wretched leper each time the memories of some sad events of his boyhood overwhelmed his mind. In the absence of such, he could be normal, determined focused and strong-willed. There was a particular time in his cadet days when these sad memories overwhelmed him so much that he felt like harming himself inside his room as he was alone. But the thought and consideration of a better tomorrow restrained him.

Zamuna could not bear her pains for a long time before she became retaliatory. She gradually began to develop and try her own muscles too, so that she would not be killed untimely. That made their home to be turned into a battle-ground of sorts, where quarrel, violence, hatred and treachery dominated. All these moulded Shigaro's childhood as he watched them day after day.

He would never forget the day he returned from their neighbourhood to see his father bleeding through his ears and nose as he lay on their bare mud floor. Out of anger and frustration, Zamuna had targeted Genje's medulla oblongata with a sizeable club. She reasoned that he had deliberately denied her security, sex and solace in their home for too long a time. So, when she could no longer contain her emotions, she turned restive and rebellious.

The day was Friday and the period was evening—a normal, cool evening. Zamuna and her two tender sons had gone almost completely hungry for three days, without any positive response from Genje. He would rather return home in the evening with a tooth-pick in-between his lips—clear evidence that he had eaten to his satisfaction from a ramshackle restaurant and bar he usually patronized. It was called London Restaurant. The first thing that greeted you on sighting the restaurant was its signpost—small, wooden and rectangular, with the drawing of a goat's head and neck and a strong hand passing a sharp *daga* knife with a gleaming blade, through the neck of the goat as it was being slaughtered. Then there was a plate of steaming fresh pepper-soup with two spoons inserted into it as it sat near the goat's head. Two inscriptions were clearly written on the signpost- one at the top, one at the bottom. The one at the top was hand-written with blue emulsion paint against the black background of the board. And it read: WELCOME TO LONDON RESTAURANT, while the one at the bottom was also handwritten, but with bright red emulsion paint, just like the drawings. It read: *Pay as You Eat*! The signpost was hoisted with a wooden pole on an elevated sandy ground in front of the building and was usually touched by some of the patrons as they entered the one sitting room restaurant and bar. It contained four wide wooden rectangular tables covered with blue cellophane as tablecloth, with two wooden benches serving each of the tables. Beside the threshold of an adjoining room was a rough liquor cabinet that contained assorted types of alcohol. Then there was Madam London the proprietress; as flashy as the city of London. She was plump, fair and pretty, with well-rounded swinging hips which a number of her patrons, like Genje, usually came to behold as they drank and ate pepper-soup.

Madam London's hair was usually jerry-coiled, and her blouses often designed in such a way as to expose part of her boobs which had remained strong and standing like that of a twenty-two year old unmolested virgin, despite the fact that they had fed two boys and a girl, and that she was already in her early forties as a single mother. She saw those boobs as her assets and took full advantage of them to enslave some men whose wives' boobs had already sagged. It was such that even when some did not have the money to come for drinks, they would still come to sit down in quietness to observe her swinging rotund hips, her partly exposed standing boobs and her flashy lips which she usually polished crimson red or yellowish-orange, depending on the type of cloth she wore and the colour of her necklace and ear rings. She was a dressing-conscious woman. Madam London knew the tricks of her trade and used everything she had as a woman for her advantage. Her voice was smoother than oil and she would alter her normal movement to shake and wobble the two lobes of her buttocks thoroughly each time she came out by herself to serve drinks or pepper-soup to some men. On one of such occasions, Genje struck her buttocks, as they swung, with his bare palm in a joking manner, reasoning that if she would not allow him to see what was inside it, he would, at least, touch it from the outside. She did not resist him as she merely smiled and swung into motion. There were only two people in that village Madam London usually permitted to see what was inside. One of them was a retired major who commanded a battalion during the Nigerian Civil War while the other was a home-based successful businessman in the grocery trade. Both men were tall, materially comfortable and good- looking.

As Genje returned from London Restaurant that evening and saw his family hunger-stricken, he remained remorseless. Shigaro had gone to the neighbourhood to see if the hope of eating a good meal could be realised. But his hope was dashed. Despite all his overtures to that effect, no one gave him anything to eat. It pained Shigaro more because he had met the particular family he visited eating. So he really met them at the right time, yet nobody considered him worthy to be given a piece of boiled yam dipped in palm oil. He swallowed his saliva and left as he came, his stomach still rumbling in anger. Zamuna had concluded to end the whole mess that day. So when Genje returned home brandishing a tooth- pick in his usual manner and was about entering their house, Zamuna picked a sizeable club and acted swiftly. Had the club gotten to its aimed target, Genje would have been as good as dead. But luck was on his side that day. As soon as he collapsed on the floor, Zamuna fled with Konja, their second son. The little Konja cleaved to her mother's back as a baby monkey would do at the back of his mother when the owner of a ripe bunch of banana they were stealing was sighted. As the mother would jump from tree to tree, escaping to safety, the monkey would grip her back firmly. Konja held tightly to his mother as she fled, thinking that Genje was already dead. She left with nothing except a piece of boiled white yam she would give to her child if he cried much for hunger. Meanwhile, she herself was dying of the same hunger.

From that time onwards, Zamuna hated all men with passion. She never again allowed any man to come close to her until she died. While she fled, she could not consider her paternal home a safe place to go because her own parents were no longer alive. Poverty and diseases had demanded for their lives two years earlier, and had actually succeeded in snatching them away. Also, considering the type of uncles she had, Zamuna knew that nobody would really welcome her back; nobody would genuinely listen to her ugly story and truly feel her pains alongside with her. Yet that was what she needed at the moment. But she knew that she would not get it from them. She knew that the best they could do for her was to allow her to pass a night or two in the compound. Then they would chase her back with whips if she dared to prove stubborn by refusing to return to her husband's house. Zamuna did not want to risk that. She decided to rather search for the house of her old time female pal; someone she believed would truly share her feelings, her pains. But it had been long they lost contact with each other.

As she ran with her son to Zima, a neighbouring town to Dakowa, their own community, in search of her good old time friend, Zamuna's strength sagged steadily in exhaustion. Eventually, she came across a house close to a mission school, where Eneza, a childless elderly widow lived. On seeing tears running down Zamuna's cheeks like a flood, Eneza quickly perceived that she was a fellow woman tasting some bitter pills of life as she did. So she came to her aid, spoke to her and welcomed her into her one-room apartment.

Zamuna readily obliged. All she needed was someone by her side. Someone who would console her; someone who would feel her pulse; someone who would tell her that things would still be alright. It was there and then that she narrated the story of her life with much tears in her eyes and pains in her heart. Eneza pitied her and wiped her tears with her palm, rubbing it on her threadbare wrapper. That was how they began to live together. And as day begot day, Konja began to call both Zamuna and Eneza, "My mother" because it became increasingly difficult for him to tell which of them had given birth to him. Each of them treated him tenderly as a dear mother would treat the child of her own womb. Konja enjoyed every bit of love and affection lavished on him by both women. He was their object of admiration, concern and affection. He provided a good opportunity for Eneza who had not nursed a child before to practice it; an opportunity to prove that she could have been a good mother if providence was kind enough to her in giving her a child - the child of her own womb. She saw in Konja an opportunity to showcase her hitherto dormant motherly credentials. He began to tap all the love that was bottled up in her as a woman. She loved him almost to a fault. Eneza would have even preferred it if Konja were a little baby boy, so that she could as well practice breastfeeding him in Zamuna's absence. That, she thought, would have given her greater joy. But Konja had been weaned already. Nevertheless, she was still happy having him under her roof because he made her feel like a mother—a real mother. He almost became an idol to her.

Eneza's pilgrimage on earth was bedevilled with pains and sorrows. That was one reason why she felt relieved to eventually have a child under her roof to tender. She had many sad stories to tell. Eneza was eighteen years old when she got married to a teacher who happened to have taught her in primary school. Somaje loved her so dearly; and they had a fantastic relationship at the beginning. As soon as they got married, it became a habit for the couple to eat every meal together, from the same plate. It was such that if one was away, the other was ready to remain hungry, waiting until the other partner returned. Then they could have their meal together with smiles and fun. They were knitted together and bonded with true love. But after fifteen years of childlessness, Eneza ran out of favour with her husband. Somaje got married to another woman who gave birth to a bouncing baby boy nine months after he first saw her nakedness. So Eneza was branded a witch and thrown out of her matrimonial home. That was how she came to embrace pitch bitterness in her rented room in Zima. And she never saw Somaje's face again until he died.

She would sit in her lonely room brooding and mourning, sometimes refusing to eat for several days. She would curse the day she was born and the laps that nurtured her into a woman. Bad world! If she was going to be childless as a woman, why didn't she come to the world as a man? Why was she sent to the world as a woman only to be denied the joy of womanhood? Why was her consent not sought before serving her such a sorrowful dish of fate? Why didn't that unseen contractor of the routes of mankind consult her before choosing such an unpleasant route for her? Bad world! Why would life prefer to handle her so roughly? Why should life be a long and pleasurable excursion for some people; a beautiful place where birds sing on trees some fine melodies for the road user who revel in a seemingly endless sunshine, and at the same time a hazardous footpath littered with broken bottles and nails for some others? Eneza brooded and questioned many things about life.

When two members of a hand-clapping, tongue-talking Pentecostal church in the town came and preached to her, Eneza began to attend their weekly activities. From that time, she was often the first person to come for prayer meetings and Bible studies. That seemed to have considerably relieved her of her sorrows as she prayed and listened to the infallible word of God. It was like the appropriate medicine which cured her loneliness and sorrows, having also found some concerned people to relate with. Eneza would, sometimes, sit in the church for hours without desiring to go home, even when programmes had ended. That was before Zamuna and her son came to live with her.

Two months into her attending the church's activities, the two sisters who converted her to her new faith developed a special interest in her and began to pay her more regular visits. They would preach, encourage and pray for her, sometimes bringing her some food, clothes and money. Eneza always enjoyed their visits. She was greatly thrilled to hear from them and from the Bible that God still loved her despite her childlessness. The story of Hannah in the Bible was of particular interest and encouragement to her. The two sisters would take a lot of time to speak and illustrate every bit of Hannah's experience as if that portion of the Bible was specifically written for Eneza. They would narrate to her how Hannah was married to her husband Elkanah who also loved her as dearly as

Somaje loved Eneza at the beginning. But Hannah could not conceive a baby for several years. For this reason, Hannah wept, fasted and prayed for divine intervention.

Each time they went to Shiloh to offer their yearly family sacrifices and to worship God in his sanctuary, Hannah would continue to cry to God for a child. Peninnah, her co-wife, did not help matters at all. She rather preferred to torment and humiliate Hannah with her words and deeds. One day, they said, when they had finished eating a sacrificial meal in the house of God in Shiloh, Hannah got up and went to pray. Eli the priest was sitting at his place beside the entrance of the house of God. When Hannah knelt down and began to pray, she was in deep sorrow, and as a result cried bitterly in her heart. Her lips were moving but her words of prayer were not heard. So Eli thought that she had taken a lot of alcohol and was drunk. They explained that Eli reprimanded Hannah, telling her to desist from her attitude of drunkenness. Hannah denied being drunk. She said that she was pouring out her heart to God as a result of her misery. So Eli blessed her, asking that God would grant her request.

Meanwhile, Hannah had made a vow to God in her prayer; that if God would give her a son, she would dedicate him back to Him, to serve Him all the days of his life. She promised God that no razor would touch the child's hair, that he would be a Nazarene—a holy man of God. God answered her prayer and gave her a son whom she named Samuel. Hannah sang for joy, expressing her utmost gratitude to the Almighty God, the true giver of children. When Samuel was weaned, Hannah took him back to the house of God in Shiloh where he lived to serve God as Hannah had vowed. Samuel later became a great priest, prophet and judge in Israel.

It was an interesting story to Eneza. Sisters Ruth and Naomi did not skip any detail of it. If one was narrating it, the other would occasionally nod her head in affirmation. They would tell her that no matter the number of children any woman had on earth, she would know nothing about them as soon as the cold hands of death snatched her from the world. In heaven, they would say, there would be no marriage and, therefore, no child to own. Eneza was greatly consoled to hear that even if she had no children on earth, God would still accept her soul at death, into His eternal bliss, if she remained faithful to Him and kept herself from sin while she lived in the world of sin. Sometimes, Eneza would sit alone in her room fantasising over those words while clutching a copy of the New King James Bible the two sisters contributed money to buy for her. She was sufficiently literate, having stopped her education at Junior Secondary School level. So she read the Bible voraciously and drew succour from it day after day. Eneza would, sometimes smile childishly at herself while imagining the inconceivable beauty of heaven; the expansive, glorious abode of God which Sisters Ruth and Naomi had also told her had streets made of pure gold, and that innumerable company of angels bow down to Him ceaselessly in those places. She thought of living there with God someday, so that she could touch the pure gold and join the holy angles to worship God in a place where the memory of her childlessness would have vanished forever. A place where there would be no more sorrow; no more pain; no more lack; no more frustration; no more stress; no more death, but rather eternal bliss with the architect of the universe. Eneza made up her mind to be there no matter the obstacles.

When Genje recovered from the blow Zamuna gave to him, he traced her to Eneza's house and attempted to strangulate her. That was the last straw that broke the camel's back. Two things happened: he did not succeed in his attempt, Zamuna never returned to his house until they were finally parted by death. The relationship died like dead wood. So while Shigaro lived with his father whose carbon copy he was, Konja remained with his mother.

Chapter Three

Zamuna seriously took ill in her tenth year of living in Eneza's house. A young doctor she consulted at the community health centre said that it was malaria and typhoid—the killer diseases that had been claiming countless lives yearly in Africa. Zamuna's health deteriorated speedily, defying all available medical logic. She also tried the potency of some native herbs but to no avail. When she saw that she would not survive it, she requested to see her first son by all means. So Eneza sent a young boy from the neighbourhood to go urgently to fetch Shigaro from Dakowa. Shigaro had visited them on a few occasions before now and had stopped coming when Genje terribly spanked him on account of that.

Shigaro was coming back from school in high spirits that afternoon when he sighted a dark, plump boy sitting on a low bench in front of their seemingly deserted homestead. As he approached barefooted and tattered, he could not really figure out who the boy was. The afternoon was a happy one for him because the football team which he played in as goalkeeper defeated their opponents with five goals to nothing. Shigaro himself was an indefatigable goalkeeper. His team was working very hard to retain the trophy of the season for the third time, and the entire school community went agog in jubilation for their landslide victory that afternoon. It was the quarter final of the tournament. After the match, Shigaro was trekking home whistling and singing their popular school song:

Go down, go down
Go down to Egypt and tell Pharaoh
Pharaoh let my people go
Israelites are marching on... Let my people go
Israelites are marching on... Let my people go
Go down, go down
Go down to Egypt and tell Pharaoh
Pharaoh let my people go!

After a little while, he switched over to another song:

Little bird on the tree
Sing song for me
Little bird on the tree
Sing song for me
Oh! Little bird on the tree, on the tree, on the tree
Oh! Little bird on the tree, sing song for me!

He interchanged the songs repeatedly as he returned home. When he reached, he was a bit surprised because he was not familiar with the boy who was sitting and waiting. Genje, his father, had, as usual gone out to have his good time at London Restaurant. The boy had barely allowed him to drop his bag before he asked him if he was the Shigaro he had been waiting for.

"Yes, I am," he answered.

"Your mother wants to see you at Zima."

"My mother!" exclaimed Shigaro.

"Yes, your mother. She wants to see you immediately."

"Is she well? What of my brother?"

"She's well. Let's go to see her," the boy said.

Shigaro ran out with him, forgetting that he had been craving for food. Though Shigaro tried further to extract some words about the situation he was being called for, the boy refused to volunteer any until they got to Zima. It was on a death bed that he met his mother after a long while. By now, Zamuna's soul was already fully entangled with death as the invisible, cruel and cold vehicle of death had parked by her side, waiting impatiently to carry her. She was almost boarding it when Shigaro entered the room. As soon as she learnt that her first strength was around, she struggled to brace up. It was as though an electrifying force came upon her. She battled to sit up but she could not. Then she stretched forth her cold right hand, held her son's head and drew him closer in order to speak into his ears. Her voice was tremulous as she spoke, as if to complain to her son that life had not been fair to her:

"Be a man, but not like your father. If I were to return to the world, I would not marry a man like him again. I wanted joy but he gave me bitterness; peace but got pieces; protection but received pain. In place of succour, I got ridicule and denial. Now, I am going the way of all the earth - the road all men will follow someday. Do not forget you brother. Do not forget Eneza—she treated us well..."

There were still words in her mouth when she suddenly stopped. The vehicle of death had run out of patience and her ice cold hand lost grip of her dear son. She breathed her last. On realizing this, Shigaro shook her shoulder, calmly at first, then violently:

"Mama! Mama! Talk to me. Do not leave us now, we still need you. All shall be well."

Shigaro was obviously disturbed but he did not cry. He could not find tears to shed for his mother. It was Konja who cried like a baby until Eneza drew him to her chest and consoled him. But he seemed inconsolable; wailing louder and louder. Zamuna was subsequently taken to Dakowa for burial.

The way and manner of Zamuna's death left a deep scar in the hearts of her children. And it was to be a long-lasting pain. When Shigaro saw his mother's emaciated frame on the bed, he hated life and placed little value on it. What a rough world, he thought. It was after his mother's burial that he fell in love with marijuana.

Some radical young men from the community had come to dig Zamuna's grave. Two of them happened to have come with the weed neatly wrapped in white papers. When they had gone halfway into the digging, they unwrapped the weed. Those who were interested in it scrapped some portions into some neatly torn pieces of paper also provided by the two boys who came with the two fairly big wraps. From the two wraps, they made smaller, tiny cylindrical pipes. Then they began to smoke, puffing out thick clouds through their mouths and nostrils. When Shigaro sighted them from a distance, he became curious because the boys seemed to be enjoying what they were doing irrespective of the fact that they were digging the grave of a woman who had died a sad death. He got closer to see that it was some white cylindrical pipes of paper with some dry, leafy contents that produced the smoke he observed from a distance. The next day, his inquisitive heart did not rest until he met one of the boys who taught him how to wrap and smoke. He told him that it was good for his body as a man. Shigaro took to it. He still managed to pass his examinations with average grades. But he began to develop a case- hardened view about life and became fastidious, unless his heart was free from certain sad memories.

THE STRUGGLES TO RISE

Chapter Four

It was by sheer determination that Shigaro enrolled into Dakowa Primary School and managed to complete it. Even at that tender age, he observed that poverty and wretchedness was crawling in their family. So he began to question the status quo, asking his father several questions which often annoyed him.

"Papa, why is our house like this? Why are my mother and Konja not living with us?"

Genje would, at times, wonder at the boldness and eloquence of his son. Shigaro was quite precocious. His father would, sometimes, shun him, but he would not oblige; he would not be frightened. It was very obvious that he inherited an overdose of his father's strong willpower.

When it was time for him to start schooling with his age mates and Genje did nothing about it, he decided to cause sleepless nights for him. He would wake up at the dead of the night and scream on top of his voice, telling his father that he would harm himself if he continued to deny him the opportunity of going to school. Then Genje would tell him that a woman does not place more than the length of her leg on her husband; that he had no money to send him to school. If he screamed further, he would give him a dirty slap and proceed to also give him a bottle of Gamalin-20, asking him to drink it if he really opted to harm himself. Shigaro would smash the bottle of the bed-bug killer on the floor, thereby attracting more dirty slaps to his cheeks. When his father saw this level of audacity in him, he perceived danger. Gradually, he began to develop almost the same level of hatred he had for Zamuna for Shigaro. But Shigaro remained undaunted.

On two occasions, he saw some smartly-dressed officers and men of the Artillery Brigade pass through Dakowa as they went for their official assignment. Shigaro liked their uniform and admired the three dark green Land Rovers that carried them along on each of those occasions. At another time, it was the Recce chaps he saw. Again, his admiration for them was so much that he waved and greeted the passing soldiers as though he knew them before. It was from that period that he began to dream to be a soldier, an educated soldier. He dreamed to join the clique of military elites who largely controlled and dominated the affairs of the nation. He dreamed to vacate the cocoon of abject poverty; to have bottomless treasury at his disposal. Shigaro dreamed of the day he would insult money which had been insulting his family; the day he would sit on it as on a chair in the day and sleep on top of it as on a bed at night. He dreamed of the time he would demolish their amorphous house and in its place erect a magnificent glass house that would probably touch the heavens. So he wanted to first of all get education at all cost. There was that inclination in him to go to school.

At nine, Shigaro had not yet started schooling because his father was still not willing to do anything about it. So he remained at home, chasing after lizards, rodents and grasshoppers. He would groan in pains that his age mates had gone far ahead of him in school, but Genje would not listen. All he did to make him to listen to him fell on deaf ears. At his tenth year, he simply managed to take his bath one morning and followed his age mates to school, without uniform, sandals and a small chalk board. When they got to school, he wanted to follow his age mates to their classes, but they informed him that it was improper; that he had to start from the least class - one, if at all he was allowed to join any class without school uniform and writing materials. Some of them were already in primary four while others were in five. Shigaro proceeded to primary one, his stocky bare foot bouncing on the ground as he moved. They had come late, after the morning assembly was conducted and counted themselves lucky that they were not caught for lateness by the school's disciplinarian who was in the headmaster's office for a brief meeting. So they sneaked safely into their classes. Shigaro entered the class, in the absence of the teacher who had gone to the HM's office, and took a seat of his choice. The pupils all looked at him as they would do to any new comer, a strange one for that matter. Shigaro looked odd in the class in different aspects, but he did not care to know. Apart from not wearing the school's uniform and having no writing materials, he was much older than the rest of the pupils in that class, and they knew it. He was lucky that the class teacher was a very humble, patient and understanding man who neither queried nor embarrassed him for his oddness. But the teacher reprimanded him for coming late. That was how Shigaro was allowed to sit in the class, without the basic requirements, even without being duly registered. When Mr. Zingina made a roll call and was marking the class attendance, Shigaro became uncomfortable because he knew that his name had not been included. He did not know what might be the consequences. The teacher merely glanced at him when he finished calling the registered names, hoping to talk with him after dismissal.

When he later learnt of his predicament during their discussion, he made sure that he was duly registered and also bought him a small square chalkboard, with the twenty six English alphabets written in capital letters at one side of it. Shigaro was filled with joy as he repeatedly thanked the benevolent teacher. The teacher, however, told him that he could not afford school uniform and sandals because he had many children to feed, clothe and shelter with his meagre income. Shigaro began to labour for people in their farms to earn some money for school uniform and sandals. Yet he only succeeded in sowing school uniform which he used for four consecutive years, patching and mending until it became completely unpatchable and began to expose his buttocks in a shameful manner. The supposedly pink colour of the short was no longer recognisable. It had turned to an indescribable colour — something like grey, but one was not really sure. As for his white shirt, one could still tell that it was once white. But it was so obvious that it had lost all elements and virtue of whiteness. It was something like the colour of clay heated and dried in high temperature sunlight. Sandals were completely out of his reach because by the time he would feed and do other little expenses related to his schooling, nothing would remain for such a luxury. So he remained barefooted all through his six years in primary school and even half of his years in the community secondary school. As he grew up, he got himself involved in diverse menial jobs in order to survive. He fetched firewood for sale and also hunted for games which he equally sold to raise some money.

Genje also did some menial jobs for people, mostly for his personal survival. He would rather prefer to use the money he realised to, possibly, finish a carton of beer or a pot of pepper-soup at London Restaurant. And when he had finished the day's wages, he would rise up, dust his buttocks and stagger home to wait for the next day. As he staggered home in such mood of satisfaction, he would hum and sing some native songs like a trained chorister. But as soon as the influences of alcohol diminished, his fiery temper and poisonous tongue would return with full force. Then he would be ready to manhandle whoever tried to provoke him if he could. Where he could not use his hand, he would use his tongue. Some people preferred his hand to his tongue because it could make one lose a peaceful sleep for several nights. That was also why some people avoided him like a plague. Once his tongue was let loose, hell followed suit. Yet many still preferred to call him for menial jobs because if he ever made up his mind and accepted any work, he would certainly finish it thoroughly in order to be paid without delay. And one must not owe him longer than a day; otherwise he could raise hell.

Apart from being extravagant in words and in spending money, Genje also had a high taste for troubles so long as he lost his temper. He was a man of seven days seven troubles. And if he was hungry and had nothing to eat, he could multiply such troubles around himself. He seemed to have a kind of liking for troubles; to be eating them like daily meal. Genje's body would itch if some days passed and there was no trouble to make with someone. There was a particular day he mercilessly beat up a twelve-year old boy because he passed him without greetings. In a hot furry, he pounced on the boy and gave him the beating of his life. The incident landed him in a police cell where he was detained for a month, until the full recovery of the boy.

He never forgot his experiences in the cell. First, he was stripped to his boxers at the reception desk, which inmates usually referred to as "counter." Next, he was pushed into a dark cell by a hungry- looking constable. Since he had no money in his pockets to "roger" those on duty at the desk, he had to be treated as severely as they could - tightened faces, clenched teeth, menacing stare and lastly the kind of push usually given to someone perceived to have nobody to easily come to his defence and rescue. That was how Genje was sheepishly pushed into the cell. Then the "Kodo" of the cell, a sort of president, a thirty-five year old hardened criminal who had awaited or rather evaded trial for five years in the cell, ordered instantly for a sound beating to be given to him as a way of saying "Welcome." It was a customary beating given to any new person who dared to enter the overcrowded cell. Genje thought that he would die in the process when ten angr y and hungr y inmates simultaneously pounced on him with the whole strength they could muster. Genje growled repeatedly as the beatings lasted. Kodo's orders were usually obeyed to the latter and with a kind of military precision. The cell itself was a stenchy lavatory because it was in the same cramped room that all the inmates defecated and urinated inside a small black plastic bucket with a cover. One of them was usually allowed to remove the wastes for disposal once in a day. Also, one counted himself very lucky and privileged any day Kodo appointed him to carry out the assignment because it afforded one the opportunity to breathe fresh air from the outside world. Kodo, of course, gave such a privilege to those who found favour in his sight; those he considered very loyal and useful; those their continual stay in the cell had become sources of blessing to him and his Kodoship; those whose relatives visited often with good food and money; those who bowed down to him very well in the morning as they greeted him. The inmates partly used the money in their possession to bribe the police officers on duty at the desk, so they could allow sachet water, snacks and cooked food wrapped in small black cellophane to be squeezed through the bars to them whenever they needed them. Kodo was always in charge of such moves. He usually had a lion's share of every food brought to the station for any inmate in his cell, without which the inmate would be thoroughly punished after his visitor had departed. The inmates were usually allowed to do their morning ablutions outside the cell once in a week- every Sunday. That was why they usually looked forward to Sundays.

Genje suffered the greatest indignity in the cell all through his stay because he never entered into Kodo's good book; he did not have the qualifications to be included in it - nobody ever visited him with either good food or money. When they discovered his stubbornness through the things he uttered as they maltreated him on the first day, they intensified his maltreatment. Kodo watched and grinned as Genje screamed and cursed. They were more irritated when they searched his boxers and found no money at all, neither was there anything in his palms. He had entered the cell empty handed, and there was nothing he could offer to Kodo and his boys. Squeezing out his black, long *thing* from inside his boxers, one of Kodo's boys named Jakoto threatened to cut it with a razor blade if he remained financially colourless the following day; if nobody visited him with real cash. He reasoned that even if he was caught unawares and bundled into the cell, a relative or friend of his should, at least, visit him with good food the next day. But he was proved wrong because nobody, including his neighbours, thought of looking for him let alone coming to the police station with food or money. In fact, they considered his absence a blessing to the neighbourhood.

If anything frightened Genje as a man, it was the singular threat to cut his manhood with a razor blade. And judging from the fierceness of the boys, their reddened eyes, he knew that they could do such a thing without remorse. He knew that most of them no longer reasoned like normal human beings because of the inhumanity and indignity they had been subjected to over a period of time in the name of cell. So Genje went on his knees to beg all of them not to carry out the threat, telling them to be merciful to him; that he was the only surviving son of his late parents; that he was a poor man - a mere labourer; that it was just because of a single slap he gave to a small boy that he was arrested and brought to the cell; that he would not do such a thing again; that he needed his manhood to procreate, so that his lineage would not be extinct. Genje rained down those words in a twinkling of an eye and continued to say even more until Kodo commanded him to shut up; that they would not beat him any longer or cut off his manhood that day; that they would wait till the next day before they would carry out their threat if nobody brought anything on his behalf for the boys.

Genje slumped on the floor after the beating, gasping for breath. One hour later, he was able to gather a little strength to sit up. He ate and drank nothing that day even though he was both hungry and thirsty. When darkness loomed and swallowed up the entire vicinity, except at the reception desk where a dying kerosene lantern and torchlight sat, Genje was totally restless as he was suffocating. The chorusing mosquitoes, the irritating fleas and the parasitic bed bugs all made the night a real hell for him. He was a little bit relieved when the day broke and he saw some rays of light peeping into the cell.

Every morning was welcomed by the inmates with differentsongs:

We are grateful oh Lord
We are grateful oh Lord
For all you have done for us
We are grateful oh Lord!

Praise God Hallelujah!
Praise God Amen
Praise God hallelujah!
Praise God Amen

Pharaoh let my people go
Jehovah God is calling
Let them go to the Promised Land
Jehovah God is calling them

They would sing the songs with whatever strength they had, repeating the lines over and over for about thirty minutes before they would pause briefly and then switch over to their anthem:

Life may be sweet
Life may be bitter
The vulture that eats corpses
Knows not its own time
The big fish that swallows the tilapia
May be eaten someday
And it shall be no more
The stubborn housefly
Follows the corpse to the grave
The careless nanny-goat
Which goes under the breadfruit tree
May die a sudden death
And it shall be no more
The leg that moves very fast
A fast eye equally follows it
We are all strangers in the world
And shall depart some day
A day unknown to us
The world belongs to no one
It belongs to God Almighty
If you are lucky to wake up in the morning
The first thing you must do
Kneel down and thank your God

The singing of the anthem usually marked the end of what seemed like their morning devotion. The anthem was Kodo's brainchild which he gave birth to after he spent one and a half years in the cell without prosecution. It came to him in one of such moments of inspiration and reflection when he woke up at the middle of the night to reflect on the nature and meaning of human existence; about the vanity of certain pursuits and ambitions; about the ignoble way he chose for himself as a youth; and about his refusal to listen to the tearful counsels of his late mother who had died heartbroken several years ago. He was an only son among four girls and was dearly loved by the entire family. But when he was enrolled into a notable secondary school to study, he fraternized with a notorious gang of *none academic students* and rough street boys who hardened him into a steel, such that the weeping and entreaties of his mother for a change meant nothing to him until she died. His father had died much earlier on account of a chronic sickness.

Though Genje welcomed the new day with a little relief, it was not to be a very good one for him. As from 8.30a.m, some relatives of other inmates had started bringing food and money to the station to see them. And they were called one after the other to see their visitors at the reception desk. The amount of money one's visitor used to "roger" the people on duty determined how long the inmate was permitted to talk with the visitor and to breathe fresh air which was usually considered a luxury and a favour. A reasonable "roger" from any inmate's visitor could grant such an inmate an instant visa of staying longer, ranging from hours to days, behind the reception desk, until the inmate's case was sorted out. And if one, like Genje, had nobody to do such services for him, he was to remain in the cell and, possibly rot away. Genje knew that he had nobody that could show him such sympathy, and nobody really did. He was allowed to eat a handful of jollof rice brought by one of the inmate's relatives in the morning with the hope that his own visitor would come as the day dragged on. So when the food was squeezed into the cell with black cellophane, Kodo ordered that he be allowed to eat just a handful of the food, with a sachet of water. He did. Kodo's lion portion was usually delivered separately to him with a plastic plate and spoon. So while others struggled to scoop with their hands from the cellophane, Kodo would simply relax to eat his like a king he was, at least, of the cell and over other inmates. The more regular a particular inmate had visitors who came with goodies, the more he was well regarded in the cell. And, of course, he would squat behind the reception desk to eat his portion of such goodies. When Genje chewed a handful of the rice and took water, he knew that he had courted for more troubles since he would be demanded to provide his in a matter of time.

It was in the evening time that Jakoto, Kodo's second-in-command suddenly remembered that no food or money had been brought into the cell in Genje's name since the day broke. As soon as he mentioned it, Kodo shook his head like a masquerade and demanded an immediate answer from Genje. But he was speechless, mouth agape staring sadly at Kodo from whom he expected some kind of mercy or in the least, sympathy. Kodo showed none of that. He instantly ordered his boys to give Genje "a grade two welcome."

It was Jakoto who first gave him a hot, blinding slap directly at his face before others followed suit, slapping different parts of his body their hands could reach. When they were through with the slaps, Jakoto brushed down his boxers, thereby exposing his manhood again. As soon as Kodo, again, sighted the black, long dangling *thing* between Genje's thighs, he grinned mischievously before he uttered, "This one is like a tuber of yam." They all laughed cheeringly. Then Jakoto picked up a broomstick and ordered four other inmates to firmly grab Genje's hands and legs. He was at this point only gasping for breath without really struggling much with those holding him because he had little strength remaining in him. So when Jakoto eventually inserted the

59

long broomstick into his manhood, Genje only yelled and growled intermittently, without any resistance as Jakoto turned the broom stick as an experienced driver would do with a functional steering at a roundabout. When they were satisfied with the punishment, they left him alone. Genje, again, slumped on the floor as he choked for breath. When he got himself and sat up, Jakoto ordered him to salute Kodo as a way of thanking him for the treatment they had just given to him. He went ahead to teach him how to do it. Kodo was usually saluted by hitting one's forehead three times at the wall. He did as he was commanded. At the third time, Jakoto pushed his head from behind so that the hitting sounded as if a big coconut had fallen from a tall tree. Then he was given "Akataka" as his new name, his nickname in the cell. Each inmate was given a nickname a day after his arrival. For his inability to make either food or financial contributions to the cell, Genje was given the *noble* duty of fanning Kodo with an old newspaper every night. That he would do for a greater part of the night until daybreak. Twenty-nine days later, Genje was released because the man who paid the police for his arrest and detention reasoned that he had paid appropriately and sufficiently for waylaying his son. But that did not deter him from courting more troubles for himself.

Many police cells in the country were hardening grounds for people who dared to venture into them. Those who had been there never came out better but bitter, tougher and with more determination to cause harm to society because their psyche would have been terribly injured. If one was lucky to leave there alive, one would leave with some horrible infections as a result of the extremely poor, dirty and smelly dungeons, not good enough for pigs, they inhabited in the name of cells. It usually took many of them several weeks to recover their health and return to normal life, if luck was on their side. Genje became harder and tougher after he left the cell. From then, there was hardly any day he visited

London Restaurant without a severe quarrel with someone, sometimes fighting with bottles and clubs. He became a terror to behold until the day he met with death.

Six months after Genje left the cell, Kodo the jailbird was finally charged to court. After several adjournments, the presiding judge finally declared him a condemned criminal. Then he was sent to prison to face the hangman's noose.

The last straw that broke the camel's back was his participation in the assassination of a prominent wealthy politician who had a gubernatorial ambition. He was seriously preparing to run for the highest office in his state if the military's transition-to-civil-rule programme was not to be a mere dribble again. While the politician was busy making his ground-breaking preparations, an opposition politician from the same state, who considered him a big threat to his own ambition, paid Kodo and two other members of his gang to nail the prominent politician once and for all. He sternly warned them to leave no traces behind. But mother luck seemed to be against Kodo this particular time. His cup of atrocities was filled to the brim and he was apprehended by the police one month after the crime was committed. He was found and captured in a five star hotel where he went to enjoy his booty with his girlfriend Apolonia.

When Kodo and his men broke into the man's bedroom to assassinate him, they did not know that he had a twenty-four hour alert security gadget that monitored every event around his residence. He decided to install the expensive gadget when he started receiving threat calls and anonymous mails warning him to slow down and forget his gubernatorial ambition for good. But he would not oblige. Instead, he intensified his grassroot mobilization. Kodo, the audacious gang leader was completely videoed by the gadget when they entered to carry out the dastardly act; when he brought out a gleaming dagger to dagger the man to death, preferring not to shoot in order not to attract attention. That was what security operatives used to trace him until they apprehended him atop Apolonia. The other two members of his gang were jobless university graduates. One was a sociologist while the other was a geologist from a reputable ivory tower. Both of them had been jobless since they graduated from the same university in the days of Structural Adjustment Programme. They had written over a thousand job applications to no avail. When they saw no light at the end of the tunnel, they decided to procure two short guns and employed themselves. So when Kodo contacted them to form a new gang with him and to execute the ignoble assignment, they willingly followed him with their tools. They fled as soon as they heard that Kodo had been apprehended. Though he pleaded "not guilty" at the commencement of the trial, he later admitted to have collected two million naira to do the dirty job when the video tape of his actions was tendered in evidence. He was totally speechless when the tape was played in the courtroom for all to see. It was then that he saw that there was no route of escape for him. When he admitted to have committed the crime, he went ahead to finger the man who paid him for it.

He was a highly connected personality who immediately made phone calls to some powerful persons and friends in Abuja as soon as he got to know that Kodo had spilled the beans. Meanwhile, he was also the person who ensured that Kodo evaded trial for five years, hoping that he could probably secure his release by chance. In the end, the Big Man was saved from prosecution by his powerful connections. He termed Kodo's indictment a baseless and subtle blackmail designed by his detractors. He vehemently denied ever knowing Kodo, let alone sending him to assassinate anybody for him. Every attempt to bring the Big Man to court to answer for himself was frustrated by his powerful friends. He only sent his well-paid lawyer twice to represent him and to say that he knew absolutely nothing about the matter. When the presiding judge insisted on having him in person in the court room, he got countless threat calls from some powerful persons, which got him out of his wits. The judge surrendered and dismissed the case for "want of concrete evidence." One week later, Kodo squarely faced the hangman's noose.

Chapter Five

Shigaro paid through hard labour to obtain secondary education and was, sometimes, associated with a variety of offences in school. Thrice, he was fingered in connection with some missing biros, pencils, books and mathematical set. But he denied it all. He was somehow perceived as one of the rough, bad boys in school. But that did not bother him at all. He certainly knew where to get the hearts of his teachers and colleagues. It was usually during the season for sports competitions and soccer in particular. Shigaro was highly energetic and athletic; an indefatigable goalkeeper. His team would lose a match only if he was not in the goal post or in perfect physical and emotional health. So long as he was there and in perfect condition, he cared less for his own life and safety. He was usually ready to take risks in order to effectively catch or kick away any ball that could have entered the net. He was indeed a strong force to reckon with in goalkeeping. His numerous fans would hardly cease clapping and cheering so long as he was there.

Academically, he was on the average scale, but he never ceased to work hard in order to improve himself. He would leave school for several days in search of school fees by doing diverse menial jobs which he had become accustomed to at that stage. It was a struggle which seemed too big for a boy of his age, especially at a time when some of his age mates were still being pampered by their parents. Yet there was no other option for him. He had never reasonably drank the milk of motherly kindness nor really benefitted from fatherly love and affection. Genje remained irresponsible to the core and was not ready for any positive change. Among his kinsmen, he was regarded as a burden and a liability; the reason for which a number of them usually preferred to relate with him from a very long distance.

Leaving classes for some days in search of money to sustain himself irritated Shigaro a great deal, especially when he saw some of his classmates whose parents really cared for. Then he would wish that he had a different father who would, for once, show him some concern and affection. But Genje had no such thing in his agenda. His usual *counsel* to him each time he sought for his fatherly care was that a woman does not place more than the length of her leg on her husband. Then he would look away and volunteer no more words. Shigaro, sometimes, would be at a loss for a while on hearing such *counsel* before thinking of the next line of action he would take to help himself. Remembering that he had a father who seemed to have made up his mind not to be of help to him usually brought pain to his heart.

In appearance, Shigaro was of average height, stout, stocky, charcoal dark, sharp and rugged. His eyes were like a blazing furnace and his countenance as stiff as Zuma rock. He could, sometimes grin from ear to ear, especially if things were going in his favour or if he was in total control of a situation or if he had a specific crucial objective to pursue. He had a commanding personality with a powerful, earth quaking voice which boys of his age hardly possessed. He could be very aggressive, tough and unyielding, and had an irrepressible penchant to dominate his environment at all times. On the whole, Shigaro had an iron-cast persona that intimidated many boys of his age. But his temper was not as explosive as that of his father. He had some elements of self-control compared to Genje.

Shigaro's domineering propensities were usually enormous among his mates. It was to such an extent that if a particular discussion was going on before his arrival, he would immediately strive to change its direction if he did not like what was being discussed. And in most cases, he succeeded without oppositions. He was the type of person who easily dished out orders—both to his contemporaries and his juniors—which he believed must not be ignored. He also believed that submitting to the contrary opinions of his mates was a sign of weakness and femininity.

He managed to pass his school certificate examination with average grades at the end of his stay in Dakowa College. A good number of his colleagues performed marvellously well in the examination and indicated their desires to continue their pursuits in various fields of human endeavour. Shigaro's eyes were firmly fixed on a military career. When he declared his interest to enrol into the Nigerian Defence Academy for a regular course, it was not a thing of surprise to either his mates or his teachers. Everyone who knew him believed he could cope and even excel, especially in physical activities. He was so happy when he was eventually shortlisted for interviews.

A repeated announcement came through the radio, informing all shortlisted candidates to report to the Academy at a stipulated time, with a pair of white canvass shoes, two pairs of white shorts, two pairs of white stockings and a set of cutlery. In addition to all these, Shigaro would need some money for transportation and for his pocket. But he had none at the time of the announcement, and the time for the interviews was short. It was to commence in a fortnight. And he knew that he could not realise the amount of money he needed to buy those items at the period by engaging himself in some irregular menial jobs. When there seemed to be nowhere to go for assistance, Shigaro went to his father to inform him and to request for his aid. Genje, without betraying any

66

sentiments, sized him up and down with his eyes and still reminded him that a woman does not place more than the length of her leg on her husband. Shigaro was helpless and angry. It pained him so much that his own father could not, for once, identify with him in such a major issue that concerned him as a young man. He became depressed because it was now five days to the D-day, a day he had been hoping and longing to see in his life; a day that would mark the beginning of the realisation of his dreams. He had struggled so much to purchase the Academy form and to write the examination. Yet he had to do so again, even more it seemed, to buy the necessary items for the interviews, having been shortlisted, or else he would miss it all. Then all his struggles would have gone in vain. At such times, he wished for another father who would sympathise with him at such times of need; a father with the wherewithal, who could simply put a hand into his pocket and deliver some clean naira notes into his hand with a pat of encouragement at his back.

He could not sleep well that night because he did not know what else to do. Genje had once again given him a full package of disappointment and shock. He had anticipated, at least, a little positive response from him, considering the urgency and importance of his demand. It was such a time when every father owed it as a debt to encourage his son, even if it was to be a mere oral encouragement. Shigaro was sad as a flood of thoughts rushed through his mind. That same night, Genje could not return home. But that was not what really bothered Shigaro because it was not a new habit. He was already used to sleeping alone in the house sometimes. At such times, Genje would not return home to sleep and would not even care to notify him earlier. He would normally stagger home in the morning without any explanation or apology. No one even expected such from him because it was not in his nature to do such a thing. So his absence that night, without notice was not a thing of concern to Shigaro. His headache was rather that he was about missing what he considered a golden opportunity—the dream of his life which he had worked so hard to see that it came through. But that night was to be a different one—far different from what he used to know. It was to be a night of eternal silence as far as the existence of the man he called his father was concerned. Genje was to be ushered into eternity.

He was found lifeless the next morning in a deep gutter at the backyard of London Restaurant. He had gone there the previous evening to take care of himself as he used to say, having made much money that day from the various jobs he did for people and was promptly paid. He was quite happy. When he drank himself into a stupor, he could not recollect himself to go home. Neither did he have the consciousness to sneak into any of the houses of the few poor widows who still accepted him and his troubles as long as there was money in his pocket. So he slept off on one of the benches in the restaurant, snoring and vomiting intermittently. At some point, Madam London, became irritated and ordered her attendants to push him outside the sitting room. They quickly carried him and deposited him on top of the slightly elevated sandy ground, near the sign post. Genje continued to snore and to vomit both alcohol and pepper-soup which he had forced into his stomach beyond proportions. It was when dew and cold began to descend that he realised that he was not at the comfort of his bed. He attempted to search for the route to his home as he woke up. But it was difficult for him because his eyes were so heavy with alcohol. Staggering from corner to corner, he hit himself repeatedly at the walls of the ramshackle restaurant. Later on, he saw a route and followed it. But it was the route to the backyard which led to a deep gutter close to the place they usually dumped refuse. He did not know when he suddenly slipped into the gutter and hit his skull so hard on the concrete. His forehead was badly cracked and he breathed his last.

A young lady from the neighbourhood who came to dump refuse in the morning saw his dead body and raised alarm. People rushed to the spot immediately and brought him out. It was such a pitiable sight. One young man was sent to go and alert his kinsmen who came and carried his body for burial. There were no tears in Shigaro's eyes as his father was being buried. He was used to seeing tough situations. He had chosen to take his destiny in his own

hands, taking each situation as he saw it on a daily basis. The only thing that continued to bother his mind was the crucial interview he would attend in four days time. Genje's presence meant nothing to him as his absence would still mean nothing, he reasoned. He could hardly remember any particular time he really felt his presence as a father when he was alive.

It was on the same day of his burial that a ray of hope suddenly appeared on the horizon for Shigaro. On hearing that Genje had died, Eneza had come with Konja to attend his burial which was done unceremoniously. It had been quite a long time since Shigaro set his eyes on Eneza and Konja, four years or more. As Genje was being lowered into the insatiable belly of mother earth, Konja clutched Eneza's left hand and wept bitterly. Even though he could not tell much about him, he had been told that it was his own father that was being buried. He had been living with Eneza since childhood. And since his mother died, Eneza had been no less a mother. She had been solely responsible for his feeding, clothing and schooling - all from her meagre resources. When Genje's burial was over, Shigaro walked towards Eneza and narrated his ordeal to her and the need for him not to lose the opportunity. He promised not to forget her if she could come to his aid to save the situation. Eneza nodded her head in acceptance of Shigaro's persuasions. She asked him to come to Zima in two days' time. Then she departed with Konja who was still sobbing.

Chickens had not left their roosts when Shigaro trekked to the neighbouring Zima to see Eneza. Both she and Konja were still sleeping at the time he arrived. When she heard a knock on her door, she thought that it was probably from her next door neighbour. She was proved wrong when a sweaty Shigaro greeted "Good morning ma." Eneza was amazed at the young man's determination and courage. How could he have defied every fear and get to Zima at such an early hour of the morning?

"Come in, my son," she said. She waved him to a dwarf wooden seat. Konja was still enjoying his sleep.

"Wake up and greet your brother," Eneza said. Konja stretched up, wiped his face with his right palm and looked at Shigaro. He did not greet him as Eneza had asked him to do. All the same, Shigaro knew that he had welcomed him with his innocent look. There was silence as Eneza patiently waited for him to be fully awake. Then she breathed out heavily and began:

"Your mother died a sorrowful death. I am yet to recover from the shock of her sudden departure. May her wounded soul rest in peace," she prayed.

The children muttered "Amen." Konja almost began to sob immediately. But Shigaro was not moved. He had not come to shed tears but to collect the money he would use to pursue the dream of his life. So his countenance remained firm, steady and strong, without betraying any iota of emotion.

"Be a man. Don't cry like a girl. We are only talking about what had already happened," Eneza said to Konja. She drew him to herself like a baby and wiped his eyes with the wrapper she tied round her waist. By now, Konja was already sobbing. Eneza seemed to have over-pampered him over the years and he had taken full advantage of it. When he was much younger, he knew how to get Eneza to buy him bean cake, fried potatoes, *chin-chin*, groundnut cake and even *suya* whenever he needed them. All he needed to do

70

was to be in a very bad mood and then sob intermittently, allowing a reasonable proportion of tears to stream down his cheeks. Eneza could hardly withstand it, and Konja knew it. He knew that at such moments, she hardly hesitated to give him an open cheque: What can I do for you? Then he would name one thing or the other. "Smile for me," Eneza would tease. Then Konja would let out a pleasant smile that usually brought joy to Eneza's heart; to her soul, before she would proceed to make his demand available. Even when Konja played with other children in school or in the neighbourhood, he had always expected Eneza to contend for him each time he felt oppressed by anyone in any way. And Eneza would do that devotedly with all her strength if she was available. Of course, Konja usually shed such tears when he found himself in such a situation and knew that Eneza was around. In fact, Eneza found herself in a situation of near enmity with several women in the neighbourhood because of the innumerable *battles* she fought for Konja's safety and comfort. Even when she knew that Konja was on the wrong side she would still defend him with her strong words and actions if necessary. For this reason, some aggrieved women in the neighbourhood, sometimes, referred to Eneza as "the woman that fights for the child that is not hers" or "one who cries louder than the owner of the corpse." They usually said that in order to irritate her; to remind her of her inadequacy and sorrow so she could probably soft-pedal in her vehemence defence of "the boy from Dakowa." But Eneza refused to oblige.

She, however, regretted the day she went to Konja's elementary school to fight the teacher that flogged and inflicted some bruises on him for his lateness to class. The teacher had identified Konja as a habitual late comer to class and had warned him several times to desist from the ugly habit, but he would not. Konja would sleep until Eneza would wake him up two or three times to prepare for school before he would do so. And as he prepared, he would continue to drag one foot after another until it got too late. So on that day, the teacher decided to take his lateness no more. After flogging him severely, he sent him back home to tell and show his parents or guardian what he had done to him on account of his persistent lateness. On returning home with weeping and bruises, Eneza could not contain the sight. More so, Konja had said that he did nothing to warrant such a treatment. In her fury, she tightened her wrappers and asked Konja to follow her to point out the very man that did such a thing to him for neither stealing nor killing. She was ready to wrestle the man to the ground and to do to him what he had done to her son. She was already confronting the teacher before his pupils in the class when the elderly headmaster of the school who happened to be an old time close friend of her estranged husband stepped in and saved the situation.

"But you are a teacher's wife, Eneza," the headmaster started, "why would you come to my school to fight another teacher without first and foremost reporting your problem to me?" The words froze Eneza into silence, and she waited for the teacher to make his explanations as he had opted to do. By the time he was through, it was clear that Konja had been flogged for a just cause. The headmaster vindicated the teacher and took Eneza and Konja to his office where he reprimanded the boy and warned him to desist from lateness to school. Eneza apologised to the headmaster and pledged her commitment to ensure that Konja complied accordingly. That was the medicine that healed the ailment as Konja never came late again and even became more committed to his studies. Eneza ensured that he had all the relevant books and other materials he needed to succeed in school. She would rather prefer to forgo buying a wrapper for herself instead of not making Konja's educational materials or school fees available to him at the appropriate time, especially when she discovered that he loved reading books and usually took his assignments seriously.

As Konja sobbed or, perhaps, pretended to be sobbing, Shigaro stared at him in disgust. And at the same time he envied him due to the affection he saw Eneza lavishing on him, only him. He reasoned that Konja was taking undue advantage of the woman's kindness by still sobbing like a baby at his age, just because he knew that she could not help consoling him for as long as he showcased his feminine emotions. What if there was no Eneza in his life, could he not have lived? Could he not have faced the realities of being an orphan? Could he not have struggled for survival as he himself was now doing? He observed that Konja was, indeed, enjoying every bit of Eneza's affection, even in his presence. He wondered if it was an attempt to provoke him to jealousy. But he was not sure. Perhaps it was Konja's nature. Shigaro stared at him for a little while and then shifted his eyes from him and glued them boldly on Eneza. His heart was now, more than before, in eager expectation of the only moment he considered important: the moment Eneza would dip her hand somewhere he did not yet know, with a reasonable amount of clean naira notes emerging. He only hoped that she would not end up telling him stories that seemed to have no relevance to what his heart was yearning for. He managed to pretend to be paying rapt attention to Eneza's stories, impatiently waiting for what he came for. Eneza paused from her narrative, and then continued:

"My children, life has not treated me well," she further complained.

"Since I was a child, I had known neither joy nor laughter for a long time. What did I do? Is this life? My husband who once made me to know love later hated me because I bore no child for him. That was why I lost my matrimonial home for another woman. Another woman. I lost all comforts and came here to live. Then your mother came to join me. With her good companionship, I began to forget my troubles, though she was also a woman of much

73

grief. Suddenly, death came knocking at the door. It did not give us a long notice. Oh! Death you are a criminal. You are an armed robber for what you did to me," Eneza mourned.

Konja began to sob again as Eneza spoke those words. He was indeed an emotional creature. But he could be courageous and resolute if no one like Eneza was around to pamper him. His Intelligence Quotient was on the high side. He cherished Eneza's pampering; her tender, soothing words. Expectedly, she drew him close to herself again, placed her left hand across his right shoulder and wiped his eyes, this time with her bare palm. She paused and continued:

"But we must forget the ugly past in order to find a good road that leads to a better tomorrow. It shall be well with both of you. When you go to Kaduna," she said to Shigaro, "humble yourself.

Don't forget us."

Having said that, she unknotted one end of her wrapper and brought out some crisp naira notes. When she observed that it would not be enough for him, she also brought out a nearby black handbag and emptied it in the presence of the two boys. Then she counted them meticulously.

"This is all I have in this house now." She spat on them and plunged them into Shigaro's right palm, praying that the money would be profitable to him. Shigaro's face glowed with joy.

"Thank you very much. Thank you very much Ma!"

He kept saying it till he left. He immediately headed to a nearby market to buy everything he needed and even more. Eneza had provided almost double of what he needed and Shigaro's joy knew no bounds. He never expected such a level of generosity from the woman; it came to him as a big surprise. He returned to Dakowa late in the morning to take his breakfast and get ready for the journey. He was very excited as he whistled and sang

"Pharoah let my people go…" and "Little bird on the tree…" uncountable number of times. Two of his classmates he had told of his departure came around in the evening to bid him farewell.

They sat together and discussed the prospects of a better tomorrow. The next day, he boarded a vehicle to Kaduna.

DREAM REALISED

Chapter Six

The shortlisted candidates began to arrive at the Academy in readiness for the interviews. They were mostly young school leavers within the age limit of twenty whose interests had been captured by the glory of the khaki uniform and the military profession. There were those who were far beyond twenty years of age but who had sworn with their affidavit of falsehood in order to fit in. To many of them, it was a long awaited dream which had been driving the engines of their hearts.

The screening of the boys started from the main entrance 'coffin gate.' Those with bow legs and other serious body deformities were sent back home immediately, likewise those with bushy, unkempt hair. As each one was checked into the gate, he was also asked to jog into the premises of the Academy with whatever luggage he came with—big or small. One could easily see the eager faces of the young boys beaming with smiles as they shook hands with one another and exchanging pleasantries. Shigaro arrived in high spirits and luckily, had no physical deformity. His scraped head gleamed with Vaseline—his only affordable body lubricant. As soon as he was checked into the gate, he happily jogged in, grinning from ear to ear. It was a dream come true! When he initially saw the coffin designed on top of the entrance gate, he wondered at its implication. Then he remembered that his father had earlier endorsed a death warrant for him in the Academy form he filled before he took the examination. It was to the effect that if he died in the process of his training or later in his career, the Nigerian military would not be held responsible. It was clearly stated in the form and he had accepted it. He had persuaded Genje to thumbprint on the space provided for it; which he reluctantly did without really understanding its meaning. Shigaro had only told him that it was their school form which he needed to thumb print for him as his father, without any financial involvement. Genje was relieved when he heard the last statement; otherwise he would have reminded Shigaro that a woman does not place more than the length of her leg on her husband.

On understanding the major implication of the coffin gate, Shigaro told himself that he would not die but would surely be reckoned among the successful. His determination to succeed was unwavering. Thirty-one candidates were shortlisted from each state of the federation and the Federal Capital Territory. They were all excited to have made it to that particular point and counted themselves very lucky.

In view of the enormous influence of the military on the socio-political and economic life of the tottering nation, many believed that joining the military career through the Academy was like obtaining a ticket of sooner or later becoming a part of the military elite that dominated nearly every sphere of national life. So it was seen as a way of gaining an easy access to the "national cake"-hot cake.

As the boys arrived, Staff Sergeant Kiri gave the necessary directives they needed for settling down, registration and commencement of interviews. When all had been duly registered, it was time for the opening ceremony as scheduled. The ceremony was precise and interesting.

The Commandant of the Academy, Colonel B.G. Doky came in company of some of his staff officers—the chief instructor, the registrar and others who were duly introduced to the candidates. In his address, the commandant welcomed and congratulated them for scaling through their exams and arriving at that crucial stage. He stated the nature and duration of the course and also briefed them on the various stages of the interviews—starting from medical to written and oral interviews, then to the physical which was more of stamina test. The commandant enjoined them not to regard themselves yet as cadet officers until they had successfully passed through the hurdles of the interviews and tests. He stressed the need for proper conduct and utmost discipline while passing through the processes. Indiscipline, he firmly stated, would not be condoned from anyone. Then he informed them that the primary calling of a soldier was to defend the territorial integrity of her nation, even at the cost of his own comfort and life. He congratulated them again, wishing them success in their chosen career. They dispersed with excitement; speaking in glowing terms about the manner the commandant addressed them. Some said that he was a model of an officer while others simply said that he was erudite. Then the trumpet announced their breakfast. All of them proceeded to the dining hall with their sets of cutleries with which they queued up to take their meals. Shigaro was overjoyed. He took as much as he wanted without anyone raising eyebrows, and he was amazed. Yet after they finished eating, there were leftovers here and there. It was like a great and sumptuous Christmas feast to him; the first of that kind of experience.

Colonel Doky was a mercurial artillery officer who cherished his career a lot. He was profoundly referred to as a gentleman, especially among the artillery corps where he primarily belonged. He fitted into the profession like a round peg in a round hole. A first time observer would perceive him as one who would be incapable of maiming an ant let alone hurt a fly. He was fair in complexion and had a natural innocuous appearance. But he had the heart of an aggressive lion in matters of professionalism. Doky would even dance where angels feared to tread. His physical appearance always portrayed him as someone who would not touch a rifle let alone pull its trigger. Yet his records and performances in various peace operations he participated would prove otherwise. He was once the commandant of the Brigade of Guards, a radical loyalist to the power that was at that time. Doky's room was elegantly adorned with both local and international medals of military service and honour. He was always neat, spectacular and conscious of professional ethics, and was once rated as one of the best artillery officers in the continent. But he loved political power, even in uniform. He was one of those soldiers who believed that no civilian was capable of leading the nation; one of those who thought that the country was not *ripe* for democratic governance and might never be; one of those who worked hard to perpetuate themselves and their masters on the seats of power; one of those who reasoned that the country could not be rightly governed by anyone else except those belonging to their clique.

He enlisted into the Academy as a cadet officer through one of its regular courses. After graduation, his first posting was to 363 Air Defence Artillery. One year later, he proceeded to Kent to attend a Weapons and Tactics course which lasted for six months. Two years later, he was drafted to participate in the UN peace keeping mission in Lebanon and later to the Democratic Republic of Congo as a military observer, still under the auspices of the UN. He performed creditably and returned with laudable commendations. Six months after the eagle perched on his shoulders, he proceeded to Command and Staff College, Jaji for a course which he also performed so well as the number two person on the graduation list. That immediately paved way for another course in the Indian School of Artillery. There he also won a medal for his excellent performances. As a Lieutenant Colonel, Doky was appointed a military administrator of a state. It was in that capacity that he first tasted political power; he loved it and desired not to leave it any more. He began to amass wealth—making diverse gigantic and mouth watering investments in various cities, in addition to a very fat bank account in Switzerland. Within one and a half year of administering a state, he had become a multi-millionaire. He was not accountable to the masses. He did not solicit for anybody's vote to be there. It was his time to shine; his time to "chop," he reasoned. It was the barrel of the gun that placed him there and not the votes of the people. He knew it.

He was two years on the seat when their boss saw the need to reshuffle and change some of his military administrators; the need to bring his other "boys" on board to also "chop." So Doky's state was given to another soldier of the same rank with him. He also did not waste time to begin his own "reaping" because he did not know when he might be asked to vacate the seat for someone else; for yet another reaper. He made hay while the sun shone. Doky was not given another political appointment, and he considered that his removal from his previous plum job was too sudden; too early. To him, it was like removing a baby's mouth from his mother's breast milk. He did not like it. But he had no options. An order was an order and "Oga" had given it. It was from there that he was deployed to take charge of the Brigade of Guards and later to be the commandant of the Academy. Yet his mind stuck to power as he repositioned himself day after day, and patiently waited and monitored other political opportunities.

The interviews and screening of the shortlisted candidates progressed speedily though it was rigorous and painstaking. It was meant to be a thorough one, involving various aspects of human development. The oral and written tests were primarily aimed at ascertaining the intellectual sagacity of the candidates. In a way, it was like asking one to defend the ordinary level credentials tendered. Some succeeded while some failed and were promptly sent packing, unless one had a "powerful force" to defend and back him up. Anyone who had no "powerful force" behind him and failed any of the tests was immediately shown the way out of the gate. Such a person was to return no more for the set. Shigaro was successful as he moved from one stage to another, and he was so happy for that.

The various human sense organs were checked medically to ascertain their functionality and soundness. A good soldier, they believed, should have a good sense of vision, hearing, smell, feeling, and even procreation. Shigaro was astonished when he entered one of the test rooms only to meet a pretty female nursing officer who mildly touched his manhood from outside his short, to know if he was really a man or a woman in disguise. He instantly proved his worth with his lightning speed rigid erection, to the admiration of the lady who rewarded him with an official smile. Shigaro's manhood almost tore his pants as he nearly spilled his seeds in the process. He had passed the test. Those with serious impairment in any of these areas were, as usual, sent packing. There were also hematological tests as well as urinalysis. Shigaro's genotype was AA while his blood group was O+, and there was nothing alarming in his urine, faeces and sputum. So he scaled through.

The bugle would first blow at 4.30.a.m. daily, and they would assemble at the training ground for parade and other physical exercises. They would line up in their various platoons to march, jog, and run round the field several times, singing various songs:

> *Early morning jogging begin a – a - ya!*
> *Early morning jogging begin a – a - ya!*
> *You de go – o – oh!*
> *Tuwo tuwo bele!*
> *You de go – o – oh!*
> *Tuwo tuwo bele!*

Caro – o! Yellow ceci – i
Caro - o! Yellow tomato
Caro chop my money run to Joe boy
Caro say she no know me again
This world nawaa! Nawaa! Nawaa!

I no know say
I no know say
Ekaete, Ekaete carry belle
I no know say
I no know say
She don carry belle come
Ejewa James e
E – e – e James e ewa
Ewa ti ko lepo
Ewa!
Ewa ti ko niyo
Ewa!
Eje wa James e
E – e – e James e ewa

The athletic Sergeant Bilo of the Physical Training Unit was always on the lead in such physical exercises. Other senior non-commissioned officers attached to the Academy were also on ground to direct the various platoons at such times. But Bilo was often the one who received direct orders from Major D. G. Tetemu, the chief instructor. Bilo was measurelessly energetic and was always found dutiful. They would sing endlessly, switching from song to song and sometimes, clapping their hands to conform to the lyrics of the songs. Most of the songs were composed by some officers and men of the Ordinance Corps. One certain afternoon, after all the candidates were subjected to a marathon race, there were two casualties. One had collapsed and died instantly while the other became unconscious and was resuscitated the next day on a hospital bed. Then he was promptly discharged to go home to his utmost displeasure. But he had to obey. There were also the rigorous obstacle-crossing exercises and rope climbing in the bushes, thick bushes and jungles of Kaduna. The training and drills were so intense that over half of the shortlisted candidates were eventually sent back home for falling short in one way or the other. It was in one of those bushes that Shigaro saw a human skeleton for the first time. He was not moved by the sight; he was totally focused on scaling through all the tests and becoming a full cadet officer of the Academy. To him, there was no room or need for sentiments or pity. He also believed that he had nowhere to return. The already decayed body was said to be one of the candidates who came for screening the previous year. He collapsed and was lost during one of their jungle adventures. After all his colleagues returned and a roll call was made, he was found missing since no one answered for his number. That was his end.

Shigaro excelled in all the physical exercises with an air of courage and optimism. The areas he found very challenging were the oral and written aptitude tests. But he still managed to scale through. He enjoyed every bit of the junk songs. When some of his colleagues complained of fatigue as a result of some energy-sapping exercises, Shigaro would grin and say that the exercises were even inadequate and short of expectations. By now, he had earned himself a good reputation as a high flier in sports and was admired by both his colleagues and some officials for that. He was the indefatigable goalkeeper of his platoon which later emerged as the overall best platoon. Shigaro was the major brain behind the feat. He remained a football magnet in the goal post. He got himself injured on the third week of their training and screening during the final match of the platoons. In a desperate bid to ensure that he did not concede any goal in the match, he had dived a corner kick at a critical angle. Though he succeeded in catching the ball, he had hit his hand badly at the iron bar and was promptly taken to the Academy clinic for treatment. Fortunately for his platoon, the time for the game ended with that corner kick. It was a celebrated victory for the team. Shigaro bounced back for training the next morning as if he was not the one that was hospitalized the previous evening. At the end of the thirty days interviews and screening, Shigaro scaled through and was selected. He had opted for Political Science and Defence Studies.

Chapter Seven

Full training at the Academy usually began after one had successfully completed the enlistment formalities. The training was essentially a five-year intense military programme involving physical exercise and drills, weapon handling, diverse operations of war, elementary battle craft and staff duties. It was geared to test and improve their stamina, knowledge, ability to lead and ability to follow instructions. There was also the focus to broaden their knowledge through various academic subjects and disciplines, depending on the course one had chosen for himself. Shigaro's inclination to the limelight partly endeared him to Political Science and Defence Studies, though he also had a natural weakness for the science subjects and Mathematics in particular. He struggled so hard before he was able to get the lowest credit C6 in Mathematics in his School Certificate Examination.

Apart from excelling in sports, physical exercises and other trainings, Shigaro also resolved to do well academically. He knew that that was where he had his major challenge and, therefore, made up his mind to go beyond the average academic level he seemed to have been confined to—both as a pupil and as a student. That he intended to achieve by spending more time to read. So he committed his entire self into every part of the programme, knowing that each part would contribute to his rating and eventual success. When some of his friends talked about being overlaboured with much academic work in addition to their rigorous military trainings, he would rather say that a battle that was announced does not consume the cripple. He complained about nothing. When a few colleagues talked about missing their parents and loved ones, Shigaro would grin. Then he would say that the black ant had no tail and, therefore, no flies to ward off.

Initially, they did not understand what he meant until he revealed to some of his close friends that he was an orphan who never really drank the milk of parental kindness. He would also add that he grew amidst thorns and thistles of life. So he was not taken unawares by some of the excruciating trainings they were, sometimes, given. Shigaro, instead, began to develop a little cheerful and relaxed attitude to things around him; the attitude of one who had come to the place of his dream; one who had gotten the desire of his heart and was glad about it. Nobody now chased him about for non-payment of school fees. He now lacked no footwear. Feeding was also no longer a problem as he now ate good food regularly. And with his monthly allowance, he could afford to buy some new clothes for himself and give some change to his girlfriend Linda. The full responsibility of his education and training squarely rested on the shoulders of the Federal Government whose property he was and would be. He worked harder to build a successful career.

Linda and Shigaro first met in town at the middle of his first year at the Academy. It was at the entrance of an exotic restaurant where Shigaro decided to visit that day to unwind. As Shigaro was entering, Linda was coming out alone cheerfully like a woman who had gotten everything her heart desired and was not in any way perturbed by the abrasions of life. Shigaro was completely disarmed by her sunshine cheerfulness that he couldn't help it, but insisted on having a word with the charming lady. She was initially unyielding as she continued moving out, with a suddenly tightened face, until he hastened up to her, held her right hand and smiled into her countenance calling her, "My baby girl." Then she softened for him and gave him a listening ear. Within a short time he led her back to the restaurant where they had a cup of expensive ice cream, roasted chicken and drinks together. Then an intimate bond ensued. They met mostly at weekends in restaurants or other hospitality outfits close to the Academy, and very rarely in Linda's house because it was far from the institution, at the outskirts of the city. Linda too usually preferred such places than her house. She would be uncomfortable if a weekend or two passed without setting her eyes on the young, promising officer in the making. She admired Shigaro's unmovable dispositions in speech, action and appearance. He also kept to time whenever they scheduled to meet at any venue; and if he would not be available due to the demands of his studies and trainings, he would never attempt promising to make it. Linda reasoned that a young man with such inclinations was to be relied upon in any kind of relationship. Yet she did not close the door of her heart to some other men that came into her life at one time or the other, even before she met him.

The first year flew into the wind, and then followed another. Cadet Shigaro maintained the reputation of being tough, diligent and professional. Towards the end of his second year, an eagle-eyed signals officer was posted to the staff of the Academy. His name was Major Z. Z. Zazanu. He was to take over from Major Tetemu as chief instructor. Tetemu subsequently proceeded to the United States Army Engineers School, Fort Belvoir, Virginia to pursue a course in engineering which had been the longing of his heart. So he felt glad when he was eventually released to attend the course. Soon, Shigaro's unhidden professional nature endeared him to the new chief instructor who shared radical views on issues as opposed to his predecessor's meticulousness and conservativeness in virtually everything he did. Zazanu began to relate well with Shigaro as a younger professional colleague. Shigaro noticed that the new chief instructor often reasoned in like manner with him and would handle issues the same way he would have done. He was a fellow leftist radical; birds of a feather so to say. So Shigaro saw in him a perfect role model and often sought for his counsel even on personal private matters. He yielded totally to his tutelage as their relationship waxed stronger on a daily basis. Zazanu whose temper was a little bit volcanic continued to pour more of his diehard principles into Shigaro who readily absorbed them as a dry and hardened earth would do to the first rain of the year. So he was more and more moulded to a very strong and unyielding personality.

In his final year, there was a particular incident that solidified Shigaro's reputation and transformed him into an instant hero, a reference point of courage. Major Zazanu had initiated a night exercise code-named "Operation Duka Duka" for all the boys in the final year. They had looked forward to having the crucial exercise which was usually one of the major events that marked their preparation for graduation from the institution. It was a battle simulation exercise slated to take place around Kachia, near Kaduna. The exercise had come and gone successfully and they were returning back to base at 2.30a.m in a long column of ten fully loaded trucks and three Range Rovers which moved before the trucks. Major Zazanu and his orderly occupied the second Range Rover while Shigaro and four other young officers, including the driver, occupied the leading vehicle. As it were, only Shigaro had a five round pistol in his hand; he was always ready for action. They had earlier packed all arms, ammunition and equipment into one of the trucks and had just entered the city when Zazanu, with his eagle eye, immediately noticed some suspicious movements in a certain bungalow near the road they were passing through. A syndicate of seven armed robbers held sway, terrorising the residents of the bungalow and its environs. So Zazanu signalled the leading vehicle to halt, and for Shigaro to arrest the situation by proceeding to arrest the two men he could see at the moment, for interrogation. But he did not know that more of them were inside wreaking havocs. He also did not know that they were well-armed; that it was a full scale robbery incident. That was why he merely ordered Shigaro to bring them for interrogation.

When Shigaro audaciously dashed out of the vehicle and proceeded to arrest them, they brought out two short guns from their clothes and opened fire at him. He immediately fell flat to the ground and pretended to have been shot dead. He was almost caught in-between fires, but he dodged it. Then there were the screeching sounds of the trucks as they halted on getting to the area where the instructor's vehicle had stopped, each truck stopping at the back of the other to wait for orders. When the robbers saw the unfolding scenario, they took to their heels. At the same belly position, Shigaro took the legs of the two robbers, who had earlier shot at him, as they almost escaped from sight. They slumped on the ground and yelled in pains. With the speed of lightning, he rose and proceeded to where they had fallen and collected their guns. At that instant, the remaining robbers inside the bungalow rushed out to make good their escape because they had known that the situation had become too dangerous. Two of them decided to first open fire at random in order to scare anyone from chasing after them. One of them targeted Shigaro but he somersaulted thrice in mid air with lightning supersonic speed, dodging the fire pouring out from the nozzles of the hoodlum's rifle. They became confused and instantly took to their heels in utmost surprise. Then Shigaro released the remaining three rounds of ammunition in his pistol, also hitting the legs of three of the hoodlums almost simultaneously. They fell down, wriggling in pains. Then Shigaro rushed to dispossess them of their rifles before he gave a hot chase to the remaining two escaping robbers. By now, Zazanu had ordered three other cadet officers to join in countering the action. They were still crawling fast, towards the area when they saw Shigaro returning with one of the hoodlums in the firm grip of his hands. One had successfully escaped. Everyone hailed him for his daredevil courage and bravery. The entire encounter occurred in a matter of few minutes. Shigaro sustained no scratch on his body to the amazement of Major Zazanu. He was proud of him. The news of his uncommon courage spread like wild fire.

Two days after the encounter, Linda visited him with a full plate of fried rice and chicken, a cup of ice cream and wrapped chocolate sweet with white sticks inserted into them. She was happy for him and repeatedly beamed her sunshine smiles to congratulate him for surviving the encounter. He had made a proposal to marry her, six months earlier, as soon as he passed out of the institution. Linda had considered his proposal as the best thing that had ever happened to her and had told Shigaro severally, especially when she received gifts like wrist watch and money from him. But he was not the only person from whom she received such gifts, even more. He was not the only man in her life, but she had said so to him. There were Abdulahi, Benson, Musa, Ibrahim, Dogonyaro and another Abdulahi with whom she also shared her life. Yet none of them knew about the existence of the other. Shigaro was the youngest and, in her eyes, the most promising among them and dependable. That was why she gladly accepted his proposal for marriage. Moreso, he knew how to give her what she wanted on bed, more than the others, and would not be tired of it until he would see her moan for "mercy." That was unlike the rest of them that could hardly go beyond a round at one meeting before being exhausted. Linda's libido was not usually easy to satisfy, and she knew it. Nothing else delighted Shigaro and gave him a high sense of pride as a man than the moment he saw this libidinous lady *conquered.*

Then she would scream and moan joyfully and pleasurably, fixing her naked eyes on the naked thing that did her good.

Shigaro's training progressed in leaps and in bounds and his reputation soared. He remained the envy of his course mates who had nicknamed him "Field Marshal" soon after the encounter on their way to base after Operation Duka Duka. He had also moved a little beyond average grades in academics due to his relentless commitment to his studies and the penchant to be reckoned among the best. He had deliberately made friends with fellow cadet officers who were known to be intellectually inclined, and formed a formidable study group with them; choosing rather to be a participant than the leader. But in sports, drills or weapons training, he remained exemplary; an indomitable reference point, and was widely respected for that.

Chapter Eight

It was not a thing of surprise to anyone that Shigaro finally emerged as the best cadet officer of his set. He was so joyful because it, again, marked the realisation of a dream for which he had worked so hard. Being the best graduating cadet of a set was by no means a mean feat, and he knew it. He received a gold medal amidst loud ovations during their passing out parade and commissioning ceremony. He felt his head swell when his citation was read during the august occasion in the month of September. The Head of State was represented by Major-General K.K. Timbata whom he appointed Minister of Internal Affairs. In his address, the minister, on behalf of the Head of State, congratulated the young subalterns for the successful completion of their course. He further urged them to be disciplined and courageous in the pursuit of their career in the armed forces. Discipline and the military profession, he stated, are two inseparable entities. He reminded them that the primary calling of every soldier was to defend his nation from both internal and external aggression; to defend her territorial integrity. He also warned them to keep away from politics and its tempting possibilities, but rather remain focused in their primary duties. After the address of the Head of State as presented by the minister, Brigadier Jegino of 21 Mechanised Brigade was invited to deliver a paper titled "Repositioning the Nigerian Armed Forces for Future Challenges." He was analytical and direct to specifics. Shigaro watched with utmost admiration. The precision and eloquence with which the ramrod tall brigadier delivered the paper captivated him a great deal as he listened with rapt attention and ruminated over some of his expressions: Amphibious warfare...must be ready at all times...granting of corpus status...reprofessionalise the force...realistic training...modern tactics...professional calling calling...esteemed ethics of military career...the pursuit of professional excellence...cyber warrior and so on.

The colourful occasion ended at 3.30p.m with a lot of excitement and jubilation. Parents, relatives and friends were in attendance to congratulate the young subalterns for scaling through the hurdles. Linda was there with her endless smiles, showcasing her perfect dentition. Eneza and Konja, who was now in a medical college, also came together from Zima to identify with Shigaro's success story. He was glad to see them, and much more glad that Eneza came with a small basket loaded with well prepared meals. He had not expected her to stress herself to that point, but Eneza, as ever, had remained a bundle of positive surprise to him, and he was so grateful for that. Now, he was to be fully addressed as Second Lieutenant Shigaro Genje. It was like a very big feather added to his wing. Shigaro would wring his neck again and again to glance at the lone star on his shoulders, on top of his expertly ironed green khaki uniform. Then he would grin from ear to ear. It was real; he was not daydreaming. He was now a commissioned officer of the Nigerian army—a gold medallist for that matter. His heart glowed with pride. He later moved with Eneza, Konja and Linda to a nearby lodge where they unloaded Eneza's basket of surprises and really enjoyed themselves. It was there that he introduced Eneza to Linda as "...my precious mother" and Linda as "...my precious wife to be." Eneza was overwhelmed by the unexpected announcement; she drew Linda to herself and glued her to her heart as tears of joy streamed down her cheeks. Linda smiled endlessly as she communicated with Eneza the way a lovely daughter-in-law would do with a loving mother-in-law. They spoke, at times, in low tones as if they did not want Shigaro and Konja to overhear them; as if what they discussed were entirely women affairs. The next morning, Eneza and Konja departed.

Shigaro's relationship with Linda began to hit the rocks three days after the commissioning ceremony. They were together in a certain fast food spot in town, in a hilarious mood, eating meat pie, garnished chicken and two cups of ice cream, when Musa, one of Linda's man-friends, walked in to eat and saw the shock of his life. He was dazed to see the same girl who had severally sworn to him in God's name that she had not known and would never know any other man but him in the warm grip of another man, a boy much younger than him in age. He was mad with anger and could neither hide it nor pretend. When Linda told him that he was the only man in her life, he had wholeheartedly believed her and had completely given himself to her, hoping that when he was financially ready he would make a marriage proposal to her and marry her. For over one year he had dated Linda, she had eaten a large chunk of his monthly income and did not relent in making flamboyant demands from him. He never complained for once, thinking that he was making investments into his future wife. But he was wrong, dead wrong. Linda was only playing her well-calculated "mogul" game. She knew what she wanted from him and was only interested in getting it for her own good, though with her body and sweet words. Musa saw stars in the day that afternoon. He could not believe his eyes and had to remove his eyeglasses to ensure that he was really seeing well. But he was. It was the same Linda he had known for more than a year; the same Linda that had inflated his head with pet names; the same Linda that had mesmerized and disarmed him with her sunshine smiles; the same Linda that had told him that she had never known any man before and was contented with him; the same Linda upon whom he had lavished countless gifts and affection; the same Linda he had promised heaven on earth; the same Linda with whom he had hoped to build a happy and prosperous home someday; the same Linda he had decided would be the mother of his children; the same Linda that had shined every green light into his eyes, without any danger signal; the same Linda upon whose arms and chest he had found comfort and relaxation; the same Linda he had intended to live with forever to behold her sunshine smiles, perfect dentition and irreproachably fair complexion. The same Linda, yes, the same Linda.

When he had stared furiously at both her and Shigaro for a while and did not know what else to do, he brushed up the right leg of his trousers and pulled out a gleaming *suya* daga and rushed at Shigaro whom he did not know was a soldier. He was in mufti. Shigaro, again, proved his worth and gallantry by the manner he instantly dodged what could have been a fatal stab at his chest. Then he ran out in self-defence, with Musa in hot pursuit as he uttered: "*Dan bura uba, dan iska. Za ka ci ubanka.*" As Musa belched and cursed, confusion reigned because the other people there did not know the very crime the boy he was pursuing had committed. Some insinuated that he owed Musa a huge sum of money; others said that he might have stolen something important from him. Yet another group maintained that the issue might not be unconnected with woman, woman *palava*.

Shigaro was faster and smarter. As soon as he ran outside to an open space where he believed he could return Musa's embarrassment to him, he stood and waited for him. Musa was daring and fearless. But Shigaro was more daring and tactical. As Musa rushed towards him, he somersaulted, landed and leaped forward in karate fashion, with lightning speed he kicked away Musa's daga before he grabbed his throat with his left hand and then gave him two heavy knocks on his nose and mouth. When

Shigaro released him, he collapsed on the ground and bled profusely through his mouth first and then his nose as he gasped for breath. Shigaro disappeared from the scene. Linda also quickly understood the situation and immediately followed in Shigaro's steps, though in a different direction. Before the little crowd that gathered knew it, neither Linda nor Shigaro was anywhere to be found. Musa saw himself the next evening on a hospital bed and remained there for another five days before he could get himself fully. A kind stranger had volunteered and taken him there. When he recovered, he began to recollect what had happened six days earlier, up to the point when a young man he never knew before grabbed his throat and dealt with him. He vowed to daga the young man to death if only he could set his eyes on him again. As for Linda, she would have a lot of explanations and apology to make before him, before he would decide how to handle her for what had happened to him.

Shigaro was furious, very furious it seemed hot smokes of anger emitted from his eyes and nostrils. But for the fine qualities of self control, endurance and forbearance that had been instilled in him at the Academy as an officer, he could have treated Linda the way he did to Musa. Now that he was just fresh from training, he was quite conscious of these qualities, which he had been taught should be part of him, and was ready to put them into practice at the moment. So he rather gave Linda a listening ear as she sobbed and explained the next day as they met. She said that she had nothing to do with Musa; that he was just one of those men pestering her life for relationship; that she had never accepted his offers and would never do so; that she really loved Shigaro with the whole of her heart; that she would still carry his seeds for him. When she had sobbed convincingly before him, he took her words. They reconciled and embraced themselves again and Linda's sunshine smiles returned.

Two days later, they were in another fast food spot enjoying their egg roll, soft drinks and ice cream when Benson, another man in Linda's life, walked in to eat, and got a rude shock. Seeing his own Linda in the arms of another man was the least he ever imagined since he started dating her two and a half years earlier. He too had been setting aside part of his monthly income in preparation to propose and marry Linda in a matter of a month or two. Before now, Benson had often counted himself very lucky for having such a decent and pleasant girl in his life. He would vouch that she was a saint; that she had never known the route to another man's arms or bed. Benson had earlier told his teacher mother during one Christmas eve that he had met the only decent, dependable, devoted, disciplined, and dutiful girl in the whole world, and would bring her to see her at their native home at the appropriate time. She believed him and was overjoyed to hear her son qualify his wife to be with such good, endless adjectives. And when he returned to Kaduna, he told Linda that he had announced her to his mother and that she received his announcement with joy. Linda beamed her sunshine smiles to thank him. But she knew that it would not work; that she did not love him to the point of choosing to spend the rest of her life with him in marriage; that she only liked him for the money and gifts she received from him, and for the miserable affection they shared.

Linda could not remember on time to hide her feelings of unpleasant surprise and shock; to be indifferent or calm in Benson's sudden presence, so as to still tell Shigaro later that he was just one of those men "pestering" her life. As soon as Benson's eyes met hers, she quickly betrayed her discomfort by shifting her eyes sharply from him, shuffling her feet as her inward being shivered, and looking down the table, ceasing to eat. Then she froze completely. It took Benson a little while to stare at both her and Shigaro in utmost shock before he recollected himself and knew

98

what he wanted to do. "You prostitute! So this is what you have been doing. Who is this small boy with you here?!" he shouted at Linda. Then he raised his right hand and gave her a very dirty slap which sounded like a clap of thunder. Shigaro deliberately allowed the hand to land that way on Linda's cheek. He had every chance to have stopped and resisted it; he saw it coming. Nevertheless, he was provoked in his spirit at the terrible sound of the slap and at seeing Linda cry like a baby. He reasoned that he had to save his face before the rest of the people there. Watching someone else slap his girl and doing nothing about it was tantamount to impotence, and he would not accept such a tag, not before two or three of his course mates who were also there to unwind. More so, it reminded him of his sad, painful past and upbringing because that was the kind of slap his father used to give to his mother. Benson had also insulted his sensibilities by referring to him as "this small boy." To him, that was the main reason, even if there was no other, why he had to fight to defend his dignity as a man, not just a mere boy. He could not stomach the two insults: slapping his girl in his presence and referring to him as "this small boy." No, it was too much for him to bear though he had thought, initially, to probably let Linda carry her cross alone.

He sprang to his feet like a wounded tiger and, first of all, returned Benson's dirty slap to him. Then a serious brawl ensued but Shigaro was on top of the situation. He brought out the combatant soldier in him and gave Benson what he did not bargain for that day. As soon as he saw Benson's mouth bleeding, he disappeared from the scene like lightning. And from that day, his relationship with Linda died. It was also from that day that Shigaro began to take every lady for a liar; none worthy of any iota of trust. Though Linda resurfaced in his room the same evening to make some endless explanations and to shed tears, he took all her words with a generous pinch of salt and simply asked her to leave his room and never return again. When she saw the seriousness of Shigaro's countenance and words, she departed.

When Musa arrived at Linda's house early in the morning, seven days after the encounter at the fast food spot, and knocked at her door with a degree of audacity, she thought that Shigaro had probably come back to her for reconciliation. But she was shocked to see Musa staring and searching into her countenance in disgust, distrust and frenzy, demanding for immediate explanations before he would treat her the way she would never like. Linda ignored his hostile disposition and welcomed him into her room or rather their room, for Musa had contributed immensely in furnishing it. She embraced him and scratched his back gently in the process.

Amazingly, Musa did not resist her, but rather allowed Linda's body to be glued to his for as long as she desired. He had always longed for that; Linda knew. She was not in a hurry to leave him as she also buried her face on his shoulders. When she disengaged voluntarily, her eyes were full of tears which began to run down her cheeks like a flood. Musa could no longer contain it. He forgot that he had come to demand for explanations from her and that his gleaming *suya daga* was still sheathed under his trousers, and began to beg Linda to stop crying, saying that he loved her more than his mother; that nothing could separate the two of them; that she would still be the mother of his children; that he would buy her everything she needed; that he would send her to Mecca; that he was ready to lay down his life for her sake. Linda stopped sobbing as Musa's fingers travelled sluggishly and softly from her chest downwards. Then she offered herself completely. By the time Musa was through with the assignment, the events of seven days ago were totally forgotten, even as Linda's sunshine smiles returned with full intensity. The well furnished room now reverberated with laughter and smiles and hearty conversations, centring on the latest lace he would buy for her, the best food in the world she would cook for him and the numerous beautiful and handsome children she would reproduce.

Shigaro's first posting was to 16 Infantry Battalion. He remained committed to his duties and enjoyed every bit of his job. He had a good car; an elegant model of Nissan product, and was given a decent apartment to live in the barracks. He was a regular customer at the officers' mess where he also enjoyed his drinks almost every evening: chilled Stout, Gulder, Star, and Champagne, hot drinks, depending on what he felt his body needed at any moment. He had a special fervour for steaming goat and chicken pepper-soup which the cooks in the mess usually prepared to his taste.

Three years later, when he became a full lieutenant, the fuel directorate of the battalion was entrusted to his care. But he did not handle the job for long. When news filtered into the ears of the battalion commander that there was a regular inexplicable shortage of fuel, he reacted swiftly by relieving him of the job and assigning him an administrative duty. Shigaro brooded over the development, reasoning that he was removed too soon. But whatever he thought of it, he kept to himself alone.

Chapter Nine

At 16 Battalion, Shigaro got married to his first wife—a tall, slim, fair-complexioned and charming Fulani lady who had a tantalizing gap in-between her incisor. She looked every inch like a Mammy-water in beauty. Her name was Zainab, a daughter to one of the senior NCOs attached to the battalion. He was deployed to the battalion from 69 Transport Regiment where he had served as a sergeant for several years. Sergeant B.G. Mohammed had a son and four daughters who lived in the barracks with him. It was a one united and happy family headed by a loving and caring father as well as a submissive and supportive mother.

Zainab was Sergeant Mohammed's first child, and had just completed her secondary school education when Shigaro spotted her, two weeks after he assumed duty at the battalion, and indicated interest to marry her. Initially, Zainab was unyielding. But the headstrong Shigaro was not the calibre of person to give up easily when he decided on a thing. So he pursued the matter vigorously and passionately until she surrendered to him. They got married in a very colourful occasion. Then the real journey of matrimony began. Six months later, the marriage began to hit the rocks. Although she was now carrying the pregnancy of their first baby, a girl, she had made up her mind to vacate her matrimonial home as soon as her baby was weaned. But she did not tell Shigaro.

She accused Shigaro of being too overbearing, domineering, intolerant and strong-hearted for her liking. That was unlike her easy-going, cool, amiable and simple-hearted handsome father. She was more perplexed when she observed that Shigaro began to philander a lot as soon as she took in, and was not always in the mood to satisfy him sexually as he wanted. Though she knew about his numerous sexual escapades and it burned in her heart like a furnace, yet she could not confront him because she hadn't the courage to do so. Also, certain minor offences on her part became, to Shigaro, issues for vehement vexatious verbal vituperations. She reasoned that it was not something she could bear in a lifetime. And Shigaro showed no promises of change. So when Zainab safely gave birth to a bouncing baby girl who was exactly her carbon copy, she considered it about the time to leave the marriage.

When the baby was weaned, she enforced her decision. She carried her baby and some of her things and relocated to her parents' apartment as Shigaro left for work. That was the end of the marriage. Shigaro was unruffled when he returned in the evening and noticed what had happened. She successfully resisted all his efforts to bring her back to their home of troubles. Nevertheless, she told him that the baby was still his, and that he would have access to his child whenever he wanted. Though her father made several efforts at talking to her in order to soften her heart towards Shigaro, it yielded no results. He was not happy about it, but he would not compel his loving daughter against her wish.

It was from 16 Battalion that Shigaro was posted to 19 Reconnaissance Squadron and subsequently to Ikeja Cantonment. Then he was promoted to the rank of a captain. By now, a good number of his course mates who had "long legs" were already majors, and some were getting ready to move to the next cadre. In Lagos, Shigaro enjoyed life to the fullest. As a captain, he was the proud owner of a Japanese posh car with which he cruised around the city and enjoyed himself. Eneza began to reap the good she had sown; he did not forget her. She began to pluck abundant kindness which she had sown into Shigaro's life several years back. He saw in her a true mother who should be well taken care of. Apart from Eneza, Shigaro saw every other woman that came around him as an opportunist—one who came to reap what she did not sow. He considered Eneza the only woman worth his real care and regularly lavished a lot of gifts and attention on her. She had also nurtured Konja into a practicing physician. The two men continued to lavish love upon her. Eneza now became the happy mother of a successful soldier and a doctor. Though age was no longer on her side, she began to regenerate like a tree solidly planted by the riverside. She forgot her past disappointments, pain and sorrow and now embraced each day with joy and optimism as she lacked nothing good her heart desired.

It was in Lagos that Shigaro decided to make a second attempt at marriage, with Sandra — a rugged, explosive and mannerless graduate of Mechanical Engineering from Lagos State University. She was tall and chocolate in complexion and had an irresistibly attractive shape. At the very first time Shigaro sighted her in a party, he could not withstand it. He could not resist her appealing figure. So he desired to marry her at all costs. In this case, Sandra who was already in her late thirties did not resist his offer as such, having become very tired of spinsterhood. She had been involved in countless relationships and marriage proposals that broke into irrecoverable pieces. In a matter of weeks, she got married to Shigaro. In a matter of weeks, the marriage also broke into tiny pieces that could not be put together anymore. It was a marriage of two strong-willed individuals; two stubborn bulls who often knocked horns. It did not last.

Sandra was already two months pregnant when she left. She could not endure to remain until she put to bed because she hadn't such patience. Having been working for long before the marriage was contracted, she rented a three bedroom flat at Ikeja, lavishly furnished it before she packed into it. She warned Shigaro not to venture into her apartment any day since she had nothing in common with him anymore, according to her. But he was not the type of person to be dared by a woman. Sandra knew it. As far as he was concerned, her threat was not more than the ranting of an ant. He could only choose not to visit her apartment if it was in line with the decision of his heart. So he waited until he heard that Sandra had put to bed before he went in company of his orderly to see his baby and to drop some items of food and money for the child's upkeep. Sandra did not welcome them with a good face, but Shigaro did not mind. He sat in her expensive sitting room for ten minutes fondling with his baby while Sandra and his orderly watched in absolute silence. Then he sprang to his feet, congratulated Sandra for her safe delivery and enjoined her to take good care of his baby. She did not reply a word to him. He began to leave. His orderly quietly followed behind him.

It was from Ikeja Cantonment that Shigaro was drafted and deployed to Liberia for peace keeping mission. That was the first foreign mission he participated in since he was commissioned. The Nigerian battalions who were drafted to participate in restoring peace to that bruised and unhappy African nation, under the auspices of ECOMOG, were airlifted from Lagos, Kaduna and Kano. Shigaro was among the troops that took off from Lagos with the Nigerian Air Force plane named and written *Together We Shall Stand*. They were mandated to restore order to the war-torn Liberia, even though Nigeria was not yet in order. But she chose to play the Big Brother; mobilizing both human and material resources to settle disputes in diverse distant terrains of the continent. It was a noble role. She preferred to keep her own wahala at home; to pursue peace in other lands where hatred, enmity, tribalism, avarice and the senseless craving for naked power had pitched brothers against one another, and had kept them in perpetual internecine strife.

Liberia was heated to boiling point by her greedy and power-drunk political gladiators. It was a protracted tussle for power by people whose motives were far, very far from being altruistic. It was sad to observe that the entire struggle was fuelled by selfishness, sectional interests, avarice and the unquenchable lust for naked power. Taylor had butchered Doe as though he wanted to prepare pepper-soup with his flesh; as though he had been hungry for his meat, and Liberia had known neither peace nor progress. Tears flowed like a river from the eyes of the hungry and impoverished citizens. Blood also gushed out ceaselessly from their veins as various loyalist militia groups engaged themselves in battles, in a determined effort to waste lives which no man could create. It was once reported that over seven hundred and fifty mortals were wasted by their fellow ordinary mortals in a singular encounter when the battle to control the capital city of Monrovia was at its peak. Instead of giving good food and quality education to the children, teenagers and youths of Liberia, they were given guns and grenades to fight. To fight and waste their lives; to fight; fight for what they did not really understand; to fight; a fight to safeguard the inordinate ambitions of their sectional warlords; to fight; a fight to mortgage their future; to waste innocent lives; to spill blood; to increase the sufferings of the frustrated masses; to protect the selfish interests of their blood-thirsty masters. Tears flowed ceaselessly from the eyes of the suffering African child.

Shigaro was in Liberia for one year. His performance and report por trayed him as a committed, courageous, competent, coordinated, conscientious, cooperative and capable combatant officer who knew his job very well and stuck to it. He received laudable commendation from his commanding officer. When he returned to the country, he was posted to Army Headquarters.

Then the eagles landed on his shoulders. He was highly elated when the long overdue promotion finally came. At AHQ, he worked directly under Z.Z. Zazanu who was now a Major-General and a staff officer. It was yet another meeting point for the two radicals. Zazanu was a highly connected soldier. He was solidly part of the ruling clique—the powers that be. Shigaro worked closely with him. But their relationship now was more of an official one; the type that existed between a boss and his subordinate. Nevertheless, Zazanu still remembered vividly that Shigaro was his gallant cadet officer when he was chief instructor at the Academy. But Shigaro did not see in him anymore the perfect role model he saw several years ago. He was not, somehow, comfortable that the radical officer he once respected and admired was now an integral part of Nigeria's multifarious problems. Again, it had been quite long they met; time had a way of changing things. Moreover, Shigaro also now perceived Zazanu as a bootlicker; one who could do anything possible to satisfy and protect the interests of the C-in-C, even if it was against good ethics, despite the fact that he was now a very senior officer. He felt that if he were in Zazanu's position, he could look straight into the C-in-C's eyes and tell him his mind concerning any national issue, concerning the pains and agonies of a suffocating nation, concerning the numerous sanctions from the international community, concerning the dwindling economy and fortunes of the country, concerning the collapsing educational sector, concerning anything he perceived was not going well in the country. He rather observed that some of the iron-cast principles he saw in him during their days at the Academy had, somehow, faded, and he was now, a sort of conformist officer. If it was because he was now a Big Man and had a bigger stomach, he did not know. He usually had contempt for such men; men who could not stick to what they believed in; men who could not own their own minds but were being manipulated by the whims and caprices of others;

107

men who could not stand boldly to speak their minds even though they occupied powerful offices; men who did a kind of eye service; men who were ready to do anything to curry favour; who worked against their own conscience in every matter in order to please others; men whom he usually called "womenmen"; who were only men because they dangle a pair of testicles between their thighs. He had enormous contempt for such men, especially if they were highly placed. Unfortunately, Zazanu seemed to have crossed over to that group in Shigaro's evaluation. So he refused to get very close him in their new relationship as he did when they were together at the Academy.

He noticed, through some of Zazanu's private utterances, that he did not really like the abortion of June 12. Yet he pretended openly to be one of the strongest anti-June 12 elements in the military, just to be in the good book of the C-in-C. In one of such private utterances, Shigaro had clearly heard him say that Nigeria would have been better if June 12 was not aborted; if Kunle was allowed to realise his mandate; if some political hoodlums had not gone to work; if the road of democracy and good governance was made straight from that time in Nigeria, with that freest and fairest election. Yet he could not summon the liver to tell such a thing to the C-in-C. That attitude alone brought him down in Shigaro's heart, from the position of honour and dignity he had earlier occupied in it. He saw him as one who was collaborating with the ruling clique to hold the country hostage as the masses watched in helplessness. He wanted a change, even if it would not be far different from what was on ground. He wanted the C-in-C out of the way by all means because he believed that the troubles of the nation at the moment were centred on him and his determination to hold on to power at all costs.

There was tension in the land. June 12 had long been aborted despite widespread public outcry. It was like hoodlums raping a beautiful woman in broad day light in the presence of her husband who had a gun pointed at his forehead by one of the hoodlums. Then there was also a trillion human rights abuses as the C-in-C sat tight on the throne. As Shigaro observed his immediate boss daily he carefully studied military politics with a lot of admiration. That was now the main thing he cherished in their work relationship and little closeness. Shigaro reasoned that he needed such knowledge; such a close observation; such experience; such tutelage. But that did not restore the glorious position Zazanu earlier occupied in his young mind. If a student admires his teacher in any way, he will be like him in that way or perhaps more, because tutelage is the mother of continuity. And when continuity is jettisoned, society either benefits or suffers. Again, when mother goat chews the cud, the child watches. When its teeth are fully developed, it emulates the mother. Shigaro continued to observe Zazanu day by day so he could learn a few things that might be of help to him in realising and sustaining his own ambition.

The nation had been a casualty of leadership since she was born. She was bruised; she was wounded; she was bleeding. She looked like an unfortunate promising virgin who fell into the cruel hands of aggressive rapists who raped her in turns without an iota of mercy. So she bore her pains in utter helplessness. She wept as the rapists took their turns, without considering her agony—her pains. Any attempt to really alleviate some of her numerous burdens was usually hijacked for egocentric and clannish consumptions. She was like a cow owned by a vast community which ended up in starvation. Would she?

Chapter Ten

Shigaro had been inundated with offers to spring a surprise since he returned from Liberia. And he had been meticulously weighing the carrot, viewing its possibility and chances of success. He burst into his office one morning at AHQ for routine military duties but soon discovered that his heart was restless. Peace vanished from his mind as a flood of thoughts rushed through it. When he insisted on sitting down to face his job, he soon saw himself on his feet again. And as he stood up, he was still not satisfied; he could neither sit nor stand comfortably. His mind was greatly disturbed by the flood of thoughts that had inundated it for quite a long time now. He was yet to decide fully on whether to spring a surprise or not; it was not a task of convenience, the type he could just scratch his head and decide casually. No. It was like one deciding either to live or to die. He was full of life; he loved life, and would not want to see himself wasted, just like that. But at the same time, he had an ambition that had kept him restless. The enticement to make the move had also continued. He wanted to realise the dream; wanted to be reckoned as a hero, a leader or perhaps a ruler, and a statesman. He wanted power. Yet the only option he had been pondering in his heart was to get it through the barrel of the gun—the wrong route. He never considered that it could still be achieved through the ballot box and the wish of the people. He did not know that power belongs to God. He did not care to know. What bothered him most was his personal safety and not the means. The end would justify the means, he reasoned. Yet he knew that the means he usually pondered in his heart was not a noble one.

He began to stroll round his office in a manner he had not done before. When he attempted to sit down again, it was as if a black ant had targeted his buttocks and had given him a sharp sting. So he quickly stood up again and stared menacingly at the white ceiling, counting the batons one after the other. Now, as if moving to confront a source of provocation, he moved towards the window of his office, folded its curtains and opened its louvers. He began to survey the environment as if he just visited for the first time. His attention drifted a little to the beautiful lawns shaped in square, rectangular, triangular, and circular patterns; with breathtaking assorted flowers, expertly trimmed, adorning each of them. Then he began to count the numerous exotic cars properly parked in various locations in the compound. But that was not sufficiently engaging. When his eyes got to where the official machine of the Chief of Army Staff, which was also the chief of all the cars there, was parked he lost count and shut the louvers. Then he stood still, not knowing exactly what he wanted to think about. He adjusted his beret twice, then the thick green khaki belt that had gripped his waist, as if to say, "I have finally made up my mind on this matter; that something must be done; that the C-in-C must go." Then his countenance glowed with determination. He was still in that mood when a gentle knock was heard at the door and his orderly entered immediately to inform him that he had a visitor. His brother, Dr. Konja, had come to congratulate him on his recent promotion. Konja came with two bottles of Champagne to drink with his strong brother.

He had not met Shigaro since he returned from Liberia and was glad he was safely back. They discussed on a variety of issues. Konja was of the opinion that Shigaro should plan and get married since he had told him that the two other marriages could not and

111

would not work again. Shigaro's marital instability was a real source of worry and a prayer point to Eneza. And she never ceased to ask Sisters Ruth and Naomi, as well as the pastor of her church to take the matter to God in prayer. Konja himself was yet to find his missing rib. That she also prayed for very fervently.

Konja also suggested that they should start getting ready to put up a befitting structure in place of the dilapidated one they had, which was presently useless. He concurred mainly with mild nods and said a word or two where he felt highly obliged, but he could not betray even a smile to Konja's exuberantly free laughter and discussions. There was trouble in his heart. Yet it was not the type of issue he could have mentioned to his own brother—not now, if at all it was necessary to mention it to him. More so, he knew that Konja hadn't the type of heart that could contain and handle such information. He was only a cool-headed "bloody civilian." So he would never tell him, not at any stage. Konja, somehow, noticed that his brother was disturbingly calm, yet he could not query it because he took it to be part of the kind of stiffness he sometimes exhibited. Perhaps his one year constant exposure to war in Liberia had hardened him the more, he reasoned. Shigaro's seat swung left and right as they discussed. Occasionally, he would seem to be lost in the discussion and would stare awhile at the cup from which he drank. A f lood of thoughts continued to rush through his mind concerning the choice he had just made. A part of him told him that he would succeed and be the next Head of State; another part of him maintained that he might fail and go the way of unsuccessful rebels.

Shigaro lifelessly narrated some of his encounters in Liberia to his brother. It was an adventurous mission. He told him how he escaped the ambush of the "rebels" on a certain occasion; an unexpected assault which instantly claimed the lives of ten peace keeping soldiers while eighteen others were seriously wounded.

Perhaps he could have been one of them if mother luck was not on his side.

The day was Friday and the time was afternoon. A contingent of peace keeping soldiers had gone to Monrovia to receive an envoy that had come to broker a peace agreement between the ruling government and the "rebel" forces who had hitherto sworn to make the country ungovernable. When the ceasefire agreement was signed, it was unknown to anyone that the anger of the rebels was not yet doused. They were particularly angry with the peace keeping soldiers whom they accused of being too highhanded towards them. A good number of their boys, they said, were killed on certain occasions when they had open exchange of fire. It was actually said that many members of the militia group fell for the superior fire power of the peace keeping soldiers during those confrontations. So they decided to lay an ambush for them on that day in order to have their pound of flesh. And they did.

After the ceasefire agreement had been signed, the august guests departed. Then the contingent of peace keeping soldiers began to return to their base, a community not too far from Monrovia. They moved in a column of six trucks and two green Land Rovers which went ahead of the trucks. They did not anticipate any attacks whatsoever from any group. So when the aggrieved rebels opened fire on them, they were taken unawares. Shigaro who was in the second Land Rover with his commanding officer narrowly escaped death. They were still about five miles away from their base when the sudden assault began. The rebels pounded and pounded and refused to remove their hands from their triggers. But for the immediate response and reinforcement from the heavily armed soldiers from the base, more casualties would have been recorded on the side of the peace keeping soldiers. Konja was awestricken as he listened to his story.

Eneza was also another crucial part of their discussion. They agreed to pay her a special surprise visit towards the end of the year. She was one woman they would never forget because she was there for them when they needed her most. Now that they were becoming financially capable, they vowed to ensure that she lacked nothing good that money could buy; whatever she needed to enjoy her old age. They made up their minds to continuously prove to her that it was good to do good.

When they seemed to have exhausted their discussion, Konja motioned to leave. Shigaro saw him off to his car and watched him drive off. After they had exchanged waves, he returned to his office, sank into his arm-chair and was once again engrossed in his thoughts. Having made up his mind to spring a surprise, he began to reflect more soberly, carefully weighing the pains and the gains.

It was from AHQ that Shigaro had the privilege of attending a number of courses, both within and outside the shores of the country, courtesy of Major-General Zazanu who always ensured that his name was included in such lists. But that was the much he volunteered to do for him at the moment. Of course, most of Shigaro's course mates had attended such courses several years back. A number of them he would now salute because they were already his seniors. Yet he was their best graduating cadet and gold medallist at their passing out parade and commissioning ceremony several years back.

Again, at AHQ, Shigaro made his third attempt at marriage. He had learnt a lot of lessons already, and was determined to make it work this time. Juliet was a brilliant thirty-three year old lawyer trained in one of the reputable ivory towers in the country - the University of Ibadan. At twenty-six, she had already completed her studies at the Nigerian Law School, Lagos, and was working with the Federal Ministry of Justice, after her one year National Youth Service in Kaduna State. Like Shigaro, Juliet was a very ambitious dreamer; a typical career lady with a taller than life ego. She esteemed herself and her career far above everything. Even when she accepted Shigaro's proposal, she had registered it at the back of her mind that she only needed to fulfil all righteousness by getting married to a man. Her primary consideration was to escape spinsterhood; just to be addressed as Mrs. Somebody. She wanted to hide under the umbrella of marriage and be known as someone's wife. She needed it, she thought. So when a man of Major Shigaro's status came her way, she grabbed him with her two hands. But she had the tall dream of becoming the head of the Justice Ministry someday and would not want anything, including her marital responsibilities to interfere with her career and dream. When she came into Shigaro's house, their house, after they had performed the necessary marital rites, it was like two powerful husbands coming together to dwell under the same roof. No one was ready to submit to the other on any ground. Juliet was not ready to play the second fiddle; she hadn't the requisite humility, and Shigaro was ready to demonstrate his manliness. Even though he had intended to make it good initially, he now discovered that he could not help the situation. He could not bear it. It soon occurred to him that he had made another mistake, and that the journey was going to be tough again.

As day begot day, he hoped to see the learned woman change - to be humble; to be sober, sometimes, to be homely, to be a woman—a real woman. He hoped to see her put up the kind of virtue he had seen in some homely women, especially in some of the wives of his fellow officers he usually saw in the barracks. He hoped to see her respect him as her husband so that he would reciprocate by embarrassing her with love - real love. He hoped to see her manage their home dutifully in the manner of a woman; to wear the motherly virtue that endeared most women to their husbands. But he was proved wrong, dead wrong. His hopes were completely dashed into ungatherable pieces. Juliet rather became stiffer and harder as days passed by. She was not prepared for any positive change. It got to the point where if she swept their house on a certain day, it would be Shigaro's turn the next day. And if she ventured into the kitchen to prepare food today, she would remind Shigaro at night that it was his turn the next day. What annoyed Shigaro most was that as a man, he would touch his own wife under a special arrangement and with her gracious permission. He considered it *unAfrican*.

He discovered at a particular time that he usually gained easy access to her body any day he spent a lot of money on her and for the family upkeep; any day he cruised with her to Tantalizers to take some expensive ice cream, meat pie and drinks; any day they drove to exotic restaurants to eat well-prepared costly pepper-soup; any day he blindly voted a huge sum of money from his own pocket, just to buy gari and soup ingredients; any day he gave her a large chunk of his own salary to buy new suits and shoes; any day he gave her money to assist in paying the school fees of her siblings and to fuel the car of her pensioner father. Those were the times she could relax herself for him. And if he did not do those things for her for a long while, she would quickly remind him that he was already failing in his duties as a husband. Yet her own income was not to be touched for the needs of the family. No! It was his family, and he was equal to the task. Her perception of needs that deserved her attention mostly centred on her ageing mother whose hospital bill had not yet been settled, the television in her father's room that got spoilt and needed a replacement, her younger brother's sandals that had worn out, her elder sister's two children who had not yet returned to school because their father just lost his job, her younger sister's five skirts she had overgrown and needed to buy new ones, her jobless school friend whose husband died of heart attack, their vulnerable compound in the village that needed to be fenced and things like that.

Juliet was often talking, with nostalgia, about the day every wo man all over the world would be "empowered" and "emancipated" from the "wicked clutches of men." She would also talk much about decentralization and separation of power, even at the home front, rule of law, equality before the law; equality at home and fundamental human rights. When Shigaro became so inundated with her lectures, he gave her the beating of her life - to prove to her that they were not, after all, equal in strength. He brought out the combatant soldier in him which was too hot for Juliet to withstand. So she ran for her dear life. That was how things fell apart and the centre could no longer hold. Again, she was already carrying Shigaro's five months old baby. When she finally put to bed, it was a boy who was a replica of Shigaro.

Shigaro was transferred to Brigade Headquarters from AHQ to be in charge of the fuel directorate among other duties. He had earnestly hoped to become the brigade major, but the one who was already on the saddle was equally solid on the job. So he remained unshakable. Shigaro was not bothered because he was equally comfortable with his assigned duties.

At BHQ, Shigaro saw a good opportunity to make good his decision to spring the long awaited surprise. He began to marshal out his plans; listing some officers and men that would back him up. Captain Kokoma was the number one officer on his list. He knew his professional capability; that he was the stuff he needed. He knew that he would not disappoint him once he succeeded in getting him to his side. At 3.30p.m he rose from his seat in his office and proceeded to the officers' mess to cool off before returning to his house. That was when the first major rain of the year was about to embrace the earth in the month of May. He reasoned that he needed to do a water tight plot. The unavoidable

117

thought of its success or failure never departed from his heart. He sent for Captain Kokoma to meet him in his flat, where he felt that they would be much more relaxed to discuss the matter. He had sufficiently weighed the pains and the gains and felt that it was the right time to commence full preparations without any delay again.

Shigaro was at BHQ for nearly one year before he received another posting to 14 Infantry Battalion as its commanding officer. That was the first major command position he was to hold in the army. He was glad. With an entire battalion under his command, he knew that he had a good chance of success in his plot to unseat the C-in-C. And he was determined to make maximum use of it. It was also there that he, again, saw something that startled him. His predecessor, who was a prominent member of the ruling clique and his course mate at the Academy, was now a full colonel with bottomless treasury at his disposal. During one of their private discussions, he even told Shigaro that he was expecting to be appointed a military administrator soonest, and that he would prefer an oil state if at all he had any opportunity to influence his posting. The then Second Lieutenant Y.B. Gamuk was a silver medallist at their passing out parade several years back. And it had really been long since they lost contact with each other. Shigaro was astonished at his astronomical rise on the promotion ladder while he had remained a major for what seemed to him like eternity. It was not only Colonel Gamuk that had such a meteoric rise. When Shigaro became more conscious of what was going on, he observed that a good number of his course mates who were in the navy and air force had also gone too far ahead of him in the system. This intensified his discomfort and dissatisfaction with the authorities.

Chapter Eleven

The 14 battalion had a leopard as its status symbol. In action, the animal was considered as one of the world's most powerful creatures. It was adopted by the battalion as its mascot to portray the strength, peculiarity and bearing of its officers and men since inception. Shigaro settled in his mind to achieve his purpose from there. He was well-received as the new CO of the battalion by its officers and men. Meanwhile, the C-in-C continued to dance the naked dance of power as if the drummers would never be tired and the music would never cease.

Shigaro's predecessor, Colonel Gamuk was posted to AHQ as a staff officer. Gamuk's father retired as a captain after serving for thirty-five years in the army. Three years after Gamuk was commissioned, he was promoted to the rank of a captain. So father and son became equals in the force. Another three years widened the gap. The eagle perched on his shoulders while the father who was now at the brink of retirement remained a captain. He was not a regular commissioned officer. Then came the issue of who would salute the other.

The young major certainly knew that his father was already in the army for five years before he was conceived, and that it was the money he earned from service that he used to train him in school. But he was now his father's senior in the same service. The father knew the ethics of the job; that seniority was what mattered, not age or paternity. So he would stiffen before his own son at the

119

Ordnance Depot where they once served together for a year and a half. He would also not hesitate to answer "Yes, sir" to him if he had any cause to ring him. The young major would feel humbled each time his own father gave him those smart salutes or answered "Yes, sir" to him in his usual charismatic way. It was an honour he would never have demanded for, except that their common profession had made it so. Sometimes, he would deliberately avoid his father in the barracks in order to save him the stress of stiffening before him or bouncing his leg and throwing hot salutes at him. He observed that the old man would always deliberately, and joyfully too, add humour to his greetings to him as long as it was in the barracks they met. But at home, the reverse was the case. The father would automatically be in charge and would relinquish none of his fatherly powers to his son. He would enforce it and ensure that he complied appropriately. Sometimes he would order him and demand for his obedience as if he was a toddler. There was a particular instance when the young major visited his father on a weekend. In the absence of his mother and siblings, his father who had just returned from the barracks and was seated in their sitting room, ordered him to go to their kitchen to dish out his food for him. It was not a suggestion but an order. Major Gamuk had no options than to comply. He entered their kitchen immediately and served his father a dinner of *tuwo shinkafa* and *egusi* soup. He understood. He had known his father from childhood as a firm and unyielding disciplinarian. The man was subsequently posted to AHQ from where he finally retired with full benefits while his son who strongly belonged to the "important clique" continued to soar higher like an eagle.

Before Shigaro took over the command of 14 Battalion, a serious protest against military despotism and for the actualization of June 12 mandate was staged in that area by pro-democracy activists led by Shola, the indomitable, radical lawyer. That was a month before Shigaro's arrival. Colonel Gamuk was unable to handle the situation as expected, which prompted the C-in-C to order for his removal from the command.

On that day, a fairly large crowd of different pro-democracy and human rights groups: National Democratic Coalition, Pro-National Conference Organization, the Campaign for Democracy and Civil Liberties Organization, had gathered in that area to begin a mass demonstration and mobilization. The groups had vowed not to allow the C-in-C a good night's sleep any longer until democracy and good governance was enthroned in the country. It was an aggressive crowd made up of the old and the young, the educated and the unlettered, the haves and the have-nots, the radicals and the non- radicals—all manner of persons. *Newswatch, Champions, Guardian* and *Tell* crews were on ground to capture the scene. And the indefatigable Shola arrived from Lagos to lead the protest by himself. He wore dazzling white knickers, a white polo shirt with white canvass shoes to match; and then a clean sunshade. By the time the protest began fully, the fairly large group grew into an overwhelming crowd as more and more people joined them to give vent to their discomfort with the regime. As they sang both native and English freedom songs and chanted: *Government of the people by the people and for the people! That is what we want! No more dictatorship! Rugami must go! Nigeria is not a family property! We want freedom! We are suffocating!*, a serving civilian minister and his entourage were passing through the same route the protest was staged. It was an unexpected coincidence. The minister was moving to his country home that Saturday morning to attend the burial of his uncle whose pension was not paid for eight months. The man was a retired headmaster and was said to have depended mainly on his pension for survival. But for eight solid months, he got nothing because a Big Man had lodged the fund into his private account as fixed deposit. On the sixth month, the pensioners mobilized

121

themselves into a fairly large crowd and proceeded to the pensions board to embark on a hunger strike for one week in order to draw the attention of the authorities to their plight. Yet nothing positive happened. One of the pensioners was said to have collapsed and died on the second day under a hot afternoon sun at the premises of the board, and was immediately evacuated to his home. The rest lamented and cursed whoever was responsible for their predicament, and then retired to their homes in order not to collapse like their colleague. More so, no one seemed to be interested in their matter at the moment. On the eighth month, the retired headmaster was said to have fallen critically ill and had no money for drugs. Every effort he made to reach the minister for a possible help proved abortive. It was either the minister's personal assistant or secretary blocked his letters or he was told that the minister travelled to India to check his blood pressure. So one morning, the man called his equally aged wife to their sitting room, where he had sat in silence, and simply told her that he would go. Before the woman could ask him where he wanted to go, he had already slumped and died. So when the minister drove into a part of the protesting crowd, some people recognized him. A woman was said to have walked straight to the particular vehicle carrying him and spat on the windscreen. The people seized the opportunity to attempt to pour their anger on him for collaborating with the C-in-C to short-change democracy and deceive the people. They saw him as a traitor who preferred to dine and wine with a dictator who had been persistently trampling on the lives and rights of the people in a desperate bid to hold on to power.

The minister was lucky to have narrowly escaped due to the determined efforts of security personnel on his entourage. But that was not without some damage on the car that was carrying him. When soldiers from 14 Battalion got to the scene, they were said to be less severe and less confrontational as allegedly directed by their

CO, Colonel Gamuk. They used only tear gas and an intimidation strategy of shooting sporadically into the air to disperse the crowd. And they did not arrest Shola that day for torture and detention.

When the news of what had happened filtered into the ears of the C-in-C, he was not happy that soldiers from 14 Battalion handled the matter in a manner he considered too mild for their effrontery. He had expected the CO to have ordered his boys for a severe reprisal or, at least, arrest Shola and other ring leaders of the protest for punishment. Leaving them to go Scott free that day displeased the C-in-C a great deal. Colonel Gamuk's reasoning was that it was a mixed crowd and not just the core pro-democracy activists whom state security agents usually hunted like squirrels. But that could not assuage the C-in-C's anger. He wondered why the battalion seemed to have been taken unawares in the first place by the events of that day. Why did they not forestall the protest even before it began? Gamuk was alleged to have taken lightly the security report brought to his table three days before the protest. The C-in-C reasoned that he could have put his boys on standby alert, could have sent them much earlier to quell it before it degenerated to a larger proportion; a full scale protest. But for the fact that Gamuk was one of General Zazanu's good boys and a prominent member of the vital clique, he would have either been court-martialed for negligence of duty or summarily dismissed. Zazanu was the godfather that delivered him from the claws of the lion. Shigaro was brought in to take over the command because General Zazanu had put in some good words for him; that he was quite capable of handling such a scenario in subsequent times to the satisfaction of the Big Masters.

Gamuk, however, paid for his alleged sin in another way. When the names of some newly appointed military administrators were announced by the C-in-C, Gamuk's name was not included for the plum job, despite previous assurances General Zazanu had given him. He had assured Gamuk in absolute confidence that if only two new governors were to be appointed; he was going to be one. And he had no reason whatsoever to doubt Zazanu because he knew that he had the C-in-C's ears. Gamuk felt very bad because his wife, whom he had earlier told that he had been shortlisted for military governorship, had for over seven months been addressing him as "His Excellency" as they waited in the wings. She had also increased the care and attention she gave him daily, and Gamuk had bathed in the euphoria. That was why it became a big blow to him when the disappointment came. Now that it did not work out, what would his beautiful madam address him as, he thought? He was almost sick for one whole week as a result of the unpleasant development. His wife too was so disappointed that she remained indoors for a week, soon after the C-in-C announced the names of the newly appointed military governors and her husband's name was not included. She had been denied the opportunity of becoming a governor's wife, she reasoned and brooded and mourned for those seven days. Her pains also stem from the fact that she had already informed two or three of her close female friends, who were her old school mates, that she would soon become a governor's wife, and they had met together in an exotic restaurant to celebrate her in advance, with Champaign, red wine and peppered chicken. She was at a loss as to what she would tell them when they meet again or when any of them dialled her number to ask about their high hope, now that the C-in-C's long-awaited announcement had come and gone.

Shigaro was in an extreme corner of the officers' mess of the battalion sipping a glass of cold beer one hot afternoon when his second-in-command, Captain Curu came in to also quench his thirst. As he saluted his boss, Shigaro waved him to a seat opposite his. Then he ordered the mess steward to bring him a drink of his choice and a plate of pepper-soup. Curu thanked him profusely and requested for a chilled bottle of Gulder. It was brought to him in addition to a full plate of *nkwobi*. As soon as the officer gulped down the first glass of beer, Shigaro casted the dice before him in an indirect manner. He wanted to sound him; to know his opinion and thoughts concerning the nation. He wanted to ascertain where he stood in order to possibly pull him to his side.

"Captain, how do you view our dear country presently; the situation of things?" he inquired, carefully observing all his reactions.

The officer paused for a while, tucked his hands between his thighs as a dog would do with its tail in a difficult situation. Then he quietly gave his response, having sensed what Shigaro would be glad to hear.

"Despicable, sad, retrogressive, unpalatable," the captain replied as though he was singing a solemn tune.

Shigaro nodded endlessly, fixing him with a mild and friendly stare. Then he waited patiently, expecting him to speak more. But he kept calm. When he saw that his boss' patience was ready to outlive his, he tore the silence by narrating the event that took place in the area before Shigaro took over command. It was about the uproarious protest staged in the area by prodemocracy groups. When the captain saw that his boss nodded in affirmation and seemed very relaxed with his details, he spoke further like a parrot.

"Many people are already tired of this regime, and with the state of affairs. I think we need a change. We need a change if the country must be stable. I think the C-in-C is taking things too far."

Shigaro was glad that he had met the right person; one who reasoned like him. He had not mistaken Captain Curu. It was obvious to him from the first day he meet him that he was a fellow high-wire adventurist, a leftist radical who could value ambitions and dreams more than personal safety or career. That was why he decided to cast the dice before him the way he did, without spending much time in beating about the bush. He had taken his time to study the captain's personality and propensities right from the time he assumed duty as CO. So he knew that both of them were birds of a feather that could perfectly flock together. And he had just proved it right, without much hesitation; unlike Captain Kokoma whom he had to follow up with much carefulness, diplomacy and what seemed like persuasion before he gave in and pledged his support for the course.

"Do you think that any one is capable of doing anything in the present circumstances?" Shigaro asked.

"It will be difficult and very risky. You know the C-in-C is a strong man, and has no intention to quit at all. But it is not impossible; only that whoever thinks of such should also prepare for either the best or the worst," Curu answered with a blank face, without betraying any emotion, as if he had said nothing serious. Then he began to pour some cold beer into his glass.

"Can we sail together in this boat?" Shigaro asked, now fixing him with a bold stare.

Curu chuckled as if the question was not a serious one, paused for a while and then gave his response:

"Together we shall rise or sink."

He spoke so boldly, without mincing words. Then he looked at his sides as if he had suddenly remembered the graveness of his words. No one was too close to where they sat to have heard him. Shigaro shook hand with him and grinned. Then he succinctly added: "We shall surely rise. There is no provision for sinking in this course."

They were still together when Lieutenant Limoena of the Signals Corps entered the mess. He had come from his unit in Lagos to the 14 battalion area to see his mistress. He left his unit on absence without leave – AWOL, and was in mufti when he breezed into the mess to take a bottle of cold beer before returning to base.

Shigaro and Limoena first met in Liberia where they served together with the ECOMOG/UN contingent. As the lieutenant stiffened before Shigaro, he took his greetings and simultaneously threw a question at him:

"How is your unit and Lagos generally?"

"Fine, sir. But there was a serious civil disturbance in the morning before I departed."

"What really happened?"

The officer explained that Shola led another rally of pro-democracy activists to protest against widespread poverty and oppression in the land; that the protesters in their numbers carried placards around Ikeja, insisting that the C-in-C must go; that Nigeria had seen hell under his government. He also said that the protest became more serious than before because the people had heard that Chijindu and Tope—active leaders of NADECO were arrested three days earlier in their residences by mobile police men, manhandled and chained like common criminals before they were whisked to Ikoyi prison. It was the police team who had been on their tail for several days before they finally picked them in their houses at the dead of the night. That was part of what sparked off the protest rally as the news of their arrests filtered into the ears of their numerous disciples. The crime was that they never ceased to criticize the C-in-C's regime; they never ceased to make what security agents referred to as uncomplimentary remarks.

The answer to the protest rally was swift. There was an order from above that whoever was found protesting should be arrested immediately, or where protesters proved recalcitrant, soldiers should march force with force. It was an express order from above. So when soldiers from Ikeja Cantonment and the recce chaps rolled out some of their newly acquired Cobra Armoured Personnel Carriers mounted with sophisticated rifles, the protest quickly died down as if it did not start in the first place. People ran back to their houses for safety. No one was ready to die for the cause of the land except Shola who stood firm like the rock of Gibraltar, tore his white shirt and dared the soldiers to shoot him if they wanted. One of the soldiers cocked his gun and pointed it at him. Shola remained unshaken. Then the soldiers became awfully amazed and wondered what manner of man he was. But they did not shoot. They beat him up, smashed his medicated eye glasses, bundled him into their vehicle and whisked him to an unknown destination. Three days later, the unknown destination was known. Shola had become an inmate of Gombe prison. He was abandoned with bloodshot eyes as he was locked up inside one of the dingy cells of the prison.

The Senior Advocate of the Masses was also an inmate of the dreaded and crude Gashua prison during the equally dictatorial regime of the C-in-C's colleague who had a settlement philosophy. But Shola refused to be settled; refused to sell his conscience; refused to be corrupted. So he was sent to Gashua to, probably, perish with the desert climate. That was, perhaps, the worst prison condition he had ever found himself. It was one of his uncountable arrests and detention in various prisons in Sokoto, Makurdi, Kuje, Kirikiri, Ikoyi, Jos, to mention but a few. But the Gashua case seemed to be the most terrific of all.

Before he arrived at Gashua, he was brought to court from Panti, and later flown in a Hercules plane, after a show trial, to Maiduguri before being driven for another five hours to the tortuous and dehumanizing Gashua prison. The prison was constructed with mud, and was attacked every night by sandstorm and other hazardous elements of the arid region. Shola collapsed there one particular night when he could no longer withstand the inhuman condition he was subjected to. He battled for his life for several days on a hospital bed before he recuperated and was subsequently released by the junta. He refused to be subdued.

While the Ikoyi protest rally was in progress, news, again, filtered into the ears of the people that some distinguished journalists, particularly Comfort and Benjamin were also arrested in the wee hours of that same morning for their "uncomplimentary editorials" and other publications the junta considered as attacks from them. Roso House of the Guardian Newspapers was set ablaze two weeks earlier by *unknown* persons. The press building was razed down after several threat calls to some prominent members of staff of the publishing firm. Uroh Bara, the chairman of the organisation narrowly escaped death. They had severally warned them to desist from publishing their anti-government articles. But they did not oblige. So the C-in-C's killer squad kept chasing them from place to place. Bugada Shittu, a remarkable journalist, had much earlier disappeared into the storm in controversial circumstances.

When Lieutenant Limoena finished narrating the details of the subsided turbulence in Lagos, Shigaro grinned and ordered for two more bottles of beer while the lieutenant proceeded to the bar. Limoena was surprised at Shigaro's seemingly joyful reaction to his narration because, to him, there was nothing that called for any form of gladness in those occurrences. But he did not yet know why, and did not betray his surprise in any way. Shigaro pushed one bottle of beer to Captain Curu and took one for himself. He knew that the ball was gradually moving to the goal post. He knew that the most volatile and disturbing situation in the land could offer him a good chance of success and acceptability. The plot had already started hatching well.

"Now is the right time to strike," Shigaro said to Curu with firmly clenched teeth.

He grinned, lifting a glass of cold beer to sip. As he dropped the glass cup on the plastic table his smile froze. His face squeezed suddenly like that of a child who had just taken a spoonful of quinine. He supported his chin with his palm and stared furiously at the beer bottle as if he had just discovered something unpleasant inside it. Two things had simultaneously flashed through his busy mind; his unpleasant and sorrowful beginning in life, and the obvious consequences of a failed attempt to unseat the C-in-C. He knew that nothing less than death would beckon at him if the plot leaked, or if it failed during its execution. He knew that he and his co-travellers would be arraigned for treasonable felony before a special military tribunal. He knew that they would be sentenced to death and would face a firing squad. He knew that they would appear in newspapers and magazines as plotters of a failed coup. Yes, he knew it. He knew it all. But he had already put his hand into the plough and would not withdraw it. *No.* That would be unsoldierly, he reasoned. Moreover, he was optimistic that it would succeed.

As far as he was concerned, he was the next Head of State of the world's most populous black race, after the C-in-C had been successfully overthrown. He would proscribe all existing political parties and protests, change the leadership of the Petroleum Corporation and order the new management to place him on a daily allowance of fifty thousand barrels of oil, *restructure* the military, direct Julius Berger to proceed immediately to Dakowa to develop it, jail some stubborn politicians and activists and settle those who would accept settlement, create more Local Government Areas for every community around Dakowa, and then schedule a possible general elections ten years away.

Shigaro became more resolute. Then he relaxed again, now sipping his beer with relish. His 2IC, Captain Curu excused himself and left for his office after he had totally emptied his bottles of beer into his stomach and the plate of *nkwobi*. He was not bothered by Shigaro's unpleasant mood swings. He knew the stress; he knew the battles that usually occurred in the minds of conspirators until their plots had either succeeded or failed. It was like a pregnant woman who was not sure of what she would give birth to. It could be a male or a female. Yet it could be stillborn. But as long as the baby remained in her womb, her mind would be far from having a perfect rest. Shigaro dipped his right hand into his pocket and picked a piece of paper cut into a rectangular shape. It looked like a call card. He picked a biro and began to plot. He began to plot the graph that could topple the C-in-C. He began to plot in a coded language which only he could decode. He began to view how the entire scenario would look like - listing other officers he would sound and possibly seek for their support. He began to write the uncertain script. He began to plot the dangerous graph that could alter the course of history and the political equation of the giant of Africa. Captain Kokoma who was now the 21C of 5 Recce Squadron was the number one name on the list.

To Shigaro, the C-in-C was like an audacious tsetse fly which had, for long, perched on the scrotum of a man taking his bath in a fast flowing stream. If the man forcefully hit it, the testicles might be destroyed with the callous fly. But if he left it, the proboscis of the fly, in the process of sucking blood, might pierce through the testicles and still destroy it. So the man must choose either alternative - to hit or to leave it. Shigaro chose to hit with caution, so that only the fly would go, and the testicles, probably, spared. He began to thread more softly because he also feared for his life.

Shola was released from Gombe prison after several weeks of torture in the subhuman condition he was subjected to by the junta. He returned triumphantly to Lagos and still refused to be silenced. His obsession was that the country was too blessed to be suffering; too endowed to be poor, and that unaccountable leadership should give way to accountable one. His obsession was the poor and voiceless masses of the country.

131

Shigaro was in his office at 14 Battalion one morning when his telephone rang. But he was so engrossed in the plot that he could not receive the call at first, until it jangled two more times. When he glued the receiver to his left ear, it was Linda's unmistakable voice that penetrated his ears and his mind. It was unbelievable. How could she still remember him after so many years had passed? How did she get his office phone number? Shigaro's voice and face was full of surprises. Linda was also full of surprises when Shigaro did not ask whom he was talking with as soon as she asked: "Isn't that my darling?" At first, he did not know the right answer to give to her. But when Linda repeated the same question with her characteristic sunshine laughter, his answer came:

"Linda, this is Major Shigaro Genje of the Nigerian Army, can I help you?"

Then her voice changed as she began to sob, saying something like still loving him; something like whether he wanted to abandon her forever; something like being sick and in need of his help; something like being abandoned by everybody; something like still

waiting to be the mother of his children; something like not losing her shape and complexion; something like still having her perfect dentition intact. She was saying something like waiting to experience, once again, the unique methods he usually touched her; something like wanting to see and experience him again.

He was patient until Linda finished saying the things she wanted to say, and then began to sob uncontrollably, in a more embarrassing manner. He reasoned that she was at her pranks again. He paused briefly and gave a thought to what could be the appropriate answer to this old time lover. He certainly had no more affection for her and was not moved an inch by her pretentious sobbing. Yet the truth was that she was now HIV positive, ageing and frustrated, and did not want to drown alone. Shigaro's answer was simple: "Linda, that period is over!" Then he dropped the phone and continued with his plot; the strategies and tactics he had been considering in his heart. When Linda dialled again and again and again, within the same week, and got the same answer, she gave up and bore her cross. The following week, Shigaro visited a friend of his in Kaduna, in connection with the plot, and unexpectedly stumbled into Linda. She looked pale, lean, sad and miserable. She wanted to engage him in a discussion but he vehemently rebuffed it and went his way. He felt that he was too busy to be distracted. He was in the city for a serious business. Linda's appearance was too scary. Moreover, she had proved to him severally that she could not be trusted.

Shigaro was about entering his car to depart when he saw a female newspaper vendor and beckoned at her. The young lady rushed towards him, greeted and first presented him *Newswatch* magazine as if to say, "see the troubles our nation is going through. Do you have a solution?" The cover story read: THE AGONY OF THE BEREAVED, THE OPPRESSED, THE JOBLESS, THE DESTITUTE AND THE VOICELESS IN NIGERIA: ANY HOPE IN SIGHT? Shigaro paid for the magazine, collected it and did not bother to look at the other papers. When he got to his hotel room and pulled off his boots and uniform, he began to read the cover story of the magazine. Again, it was a pathetic story that could rob any right thinking citizen of his or her sleep for several days, if not weeks. The first paragraph of the story narrated how the aged parents of both Koolo and Bola Oluwa were still lamenting the losses of their breadwinners; how they could no longer afford their drugs and the good meals they were used to when their worthy sons were still alive; how they could no longer change their clothes easily; how Bola Oluwa's mother wept every night if only her dear son would return to her; how the tuition fees of Bola Oluwa's children had not been paid for two terms; how his wife and the little children had been learning how to swallow *gari* and *amala* in place of semolina since their father was wasted; how their landlord had been threatening to throw their properties into the gutter for still not paying their house rents after several months; how Koolo's father prayed for the gods of Basu land to avenge the murder of his son; how his mother mentioned the C-in-C's name several times in her state of bitterness.

The rest of the story dwelt on the general situation in the country at present. It was how some pro-democracy activists and protesters had been clamped down in suffering in various prisons and police cells; how they had been denied access to their families for several months; how their families lived daily in perpetual fear of their safety; how some of them were being starved in captivity in a bid for them to endorse that they would never protest again if released; how many graduates had remained unemployed ten years after they graduated from the universities and how their poor parents who had trained them with their sweat and struggles were terribly lamenting; how some of the graduates had resorted to armed robbery and kidnapping in order to survive; how some destitute citizens slept under bridges in Lagos and Port Harcourt because they could not afford shelters over their heads; how some of them feigned insanity in order to be given money as they begged; how a military governor in an oil rich state cornered a beautiful lady at the end of a press conference he organised, and how the same lady later became the mother of his son; how some notable men sent their *boys* to campuses to select for them girls that were much younger than their own daughters as mistresses; how some families in certain places held meetings and resolved to send some of their daughters to Italy to become expensive *ashawos*; how some of those girls slept with dogs and contracted some incurable ailments; how some people who made big money through dubious means were being honoured while honest and hard working persons were being denigrated for refusing to endorse lies; how ethnicity and tribalism had unfortunately permeated every aspect of national life and service, including the military; how some wicked Big Men sneaked about at night to impregnate some mad women in certain cities in order to acquire political power or retain their positions or to make bigger monies—one of such mad women was said to have given birth to triplets, all boys, in Port Harcourt while another delivered twin girls under a Lagos flyover. Some caring motherless babies' homes were said to have taken those kids from their "mad mothers" for safety reasons. *Mad mothers!* The writer of the story also discussed how some girls in tertiary institutions turned to prostitutes because their parents could no longer afford their school fees due to the hardship in the land; how the price of a cup of *gari* had risen so high within a short period of time; how some families were torn asunder because their fathers lost their jobs in the ministries and parastatals, and so could no longer afford even *gari* for them; how some military and civilian politicians travelled every weekend to Dubai, Frankfurt, New York and London just to spend the weekend in highbrow hotels and to treat headache in hospitals over there; how some of them dug soak away of hard concrete in their backyards and villages to hide cartons of naira and dollar notes; how some public office holders spent millions of tax payers' money in buying bullet proof cars for themselves and other exotic cars for their girlfriends; how they refused to sign some contracts until they were given twenty percent; how they put the salaries of workers into their personal accounts as fixed deposits for several months; how some of their workers died of hunger while endlessly waiting for their salaries; how billions of pension fund was being hijacked by some powerful elements; how some desperate businessmen moulded chalk in the name of Phensic and Panadol at Alaba International Market and Onitsha bridge head; how they mixed up urine and water and labelled it Aspirin; how some innocent citizens drank such *drugs* and slept off forever; how some

135

guests that checked into Otoko Hotel got missing; how some highly placed individuals collaborated with expatriate firms to steal billions of dollars in the oil sector; how some contractors refused to properly execute assigned projects but, rather, resorted to building substandard roads that were readily washed off at the first encounter with rainy season; how policemen threatened and extorted money from commuter drivers on the roads; how they allowed flashy cars that carried fresh human heads to pass through their checkpoints as soon as they were *rogered*. It was almost a completely disheartening story which ended with the question: **ANY HOPE IN SIGHT?** Nevertheless, there was a rider which read: **How Powerful Horses Conquered the World in Atlanta; The Rise and Fall of Brazilian Samba.** The picture at the cover page of the magazine was that of a woman carrying some heavy burdens of life at her back, and was obviously in agonizing pains as she pleaded for someone to come and rescue her lest she dies. The loads were so enormous that her back was bent like a bow, and hot tears and sweat ran down from her eyes and from her wrinkled countenance. But looking closely at her face, one could still tell that she was once beautiful, and that her beauty could still be redeemed if only she got the help she earnestly sought for.

Shigaro threw down the magazine and shrugged and shook his head. He breathed in deeply and then exhaled the large volume of air as he stared critically at the magazine. He would ban it when he took over so they would not use their biro to mar his regime. He proceeded to the bathroom and took a shower of warm water and then dialled one of the hotel attendants to bring him fried rice and chicken, and a big bottle of Guinness Stout. He slept off not long after he finished the meal because it was already night. In his dream, he saw Captain Kokoma rolling out five Russian made Cobra Armoured Personnel Carriers from his unit in support of the putsch; saw his entire battalion marching out with him in full combat kits for action; saw the C-in-C escaping through a tunnel that ran from the villa to his village; saw the soldiers with him overtaking and capturing him as he pleaded with them to spare his life; saw Captain Curu sweating profusely as he bombarded and shot fiercely at the villa in order to overpower the security guards on duty that night; saw himself making his maiden broadcast as Head of State to a joyfully surprised nation; saw some men and women beating drums, dancing and celebrating the successful overthrow of the C-in-C in certain streets in Lagos, Port Harcourt, Jos, Makurdi, Ibadan, Enugu, Kaduna and Abuja. When he woke up in the morning he was so happy. To him, the dreams were a clear sign that he would succeed and rule Nigeria; that he would not take the dangerous side of the coin; that all his efforts would not be in vain. He smiled like a man who had won American visa lottery and then burst into an old school song "...Go down to Egypt and tell Pharaoh..." and "Little bird on the tree sing song for me." He hurriedly kitted up after taking his showers, cleared his hotel bills and drove out of Kaduna to his base.

Shigaro returned to base and received a two-page letter written and posted to him by Eneza. He smiled when he saw Eneza's usual salutation, "My dear son" as well as the endless encomiums she lavished on him for the chunk of money and food stuffs he sent to her about two months earlier. Then she prayed for his good health, promotion and success in all his endeavours, and for "...bad belle" people not to see him. The rest of the letter dwelt on her serious concern over Shigaro's marital instability and her prayers for the anomaly to be rectified as soon as possible. It read: "...my son, I am deeply worried that you are yet to settle down once and for all with a wife, and I am praying that the matter be resolved soon...There're many good girls in Zima and Dakowa who can make a good home..." Shigaro finished reading the letter and put it inside the drawer of his table, reflected over its major content for a brief moment and then pushed it off his mind so he could concentrate on his plot. He did.

Chapter Twelve

Despite the pains and woes of the nation, a committee of paid pipers surrounded the C-in-C's table. They were numerous. Some said that he was the messiah the tottering nation had been waiting for while others whispered to him that he was an ideal leader. So they advised him to ignore his "detractors" and continue with the "good work" he had been doing. Wonderful work! And as Ghana-must-go continued to change hands, the pipers continued to produce diverse tunes of music commensurate with his payment. They used their beautiful melodies to decorate the C-in-C's ears. He loved it. They told him that the country was good and that without him as the Head of State she might not exist; that all was well; that he was the only person that was capable of handling the tottering giant and her troubles.

The C-in-C bathed in opulence, looting and *squandermania*. Billions of naira were changed to dollars and stashed away through his cronies into numerous foreign bank accounts. He also acquired several high-brow properties and investments scattered all over the places, including a breath-taking, towering glass house in a major commercial city in the country. It was said that even the trained security dogs in the villa were rich - stupendously rich; rich enough to possibly lend some money to some impoverished citizens. Every day, each of the ten hefty and handsome-looking dogs was said to be entitled to a good tea of three tins of condensed Holland Peak milk and fried rice as breakfast, a full plate of well-prepared chicken pepper-soup for lunch, and a full roll of long crackers biscuit and pineapple flavoured juice for dinner. Also, each of the lions in the villa zoo was entitled to a full-grown healthy goat or a full-fledged turkey. But the average human citizen scarcely afforded three scanty meals per day. It was once reported that the C-in-C paid five million naira to romance a young, pretty Igbo virgin; just for open and close. Indian prostitutes were also said to be his regular guests.

When the committee of paid pipers observed that the C-in-C cherished eulogy, they gave him an overdose of it, an overdose of sycophancy and flattery. It was so intoxicating to him. When a king's table is surrounded with sycophants, he miscarries justice and neglects good governance. And when there is miscarriage of justice and lack of truth in leadership, the people, the grasses, bear the brunt. Justice delayed is justice denied; and justice denied is justice murdered. There was a huge accumulation of murdered justice in the land. And the pregnant nation was stretched to her elastic limit. No one knew the baby she would deliver. It was a case of who would bell the cat?

Shigaro rose at the mess one afternoon, after he returned from his visit to Kaduna, and was fully determined to spring not just a surprise but a very successful one. His heart was filled with optimism. His visit to Kaduna was not fruitless but rather hopeful and invigorating. One of his trusted friends and colleagues Major H.E. Kekuru had given him his full support and backing, and had promised to coordinate their activities from that direction. More so, the only dream he had since he started the plot was on a good and successful note. It was on his return from Kaduna that he code-named the project "Operation Leopard Claw." Soon, the leopard would sail.

THE LIBERATING TENSION

Chapter Thirteen

Solidarity forever! Solidarity forever! Solidarity forever!
We shall always fight our course
Soli! Soli! Soli!

They sang it, they chanted it. They demonstrated and displayed it with diverse inscriptions boldly written on the placards they carried. Some of the placards read:

"RUGAMI MUST GO!"

"WE ARE TIRED OF MILITARY RULE!"

"WE WANT DEMOCRACY AND GOOD GOVERNANCE! "

"RELEASE ALL POLITICAL PRISONERS!"

"SET KUNLE FREE!"

"NO MORE DETENTION!"

"JUNE 12 IS ALIVE!"

"CHIJINDU IS A PRISONER OF CONSCIENCE!"

"NIGERIA MUST BE FREE!"

"NIGERIA MUST MOVE FORWARD!"

It was a June 12 protest rally at Allen Avenue Ikeja, Lagos where a crowd of pro-democracy and human rights crusaders had gathered to begin a commemorative rally. Shola, Obeche, Tope— who was released from detention and torture a fortnight earlier, and other pro-democracy bigwigs were there to inspire the people.

But Chijindu had not yet been released. After singing and chanting for a while, the crowd began to move towards Ikeja Central Business District where Shola would address them. It was a rally to demand for their rights: the fundamental human rights; the right to life; the right to vote and be voted for; the right to live in their own country without being chased about by the police and the military—by the C- in-C's dangerous strike force; freedom of speech and association; press freedom.

June 12 was aborted but it was alive in the hearts of the people. That was what they came out that morning to prove and to tell the entire world. They wanted it to be realized - the unforgettable June 12; the day Nigeria had her freest and fairest election that did not survive; that did not see the light of the day. It was the day the world eagerly waited to welcome Nigeria into the league of democratic and free nations.

Apart from serving as a commemorative rally for June 12, the crowd also gathered to use the avenue to give vent to their anger over a number of things that were really going wrong in the country, particularly the debilitating poverty level and unemployment. Again, Shola was on the lead as they proceeded, now faster, to the central business district of Ikeja. He wanted to address the people before the expected would happen: before state security agents would start bombarding them with tear gas; before the police and the army would start cocking their rifles to terrorize them, and before they would arrest him for another round of detention. Or possibly poison him to death. He was prepared for it. Shola was fearless and had features harder than igneous rock. He would not sell his conscience for porridge yam. He was a phenomenon - the people's advocate; a rare breed; an indomitable force. The C-in-C and other dictators before him all hated his guts.

Three weeks before the rally, the hungry and angry labour unionists were also on the streets to protest for justice and fair treatment. Comrade Shaka had led them to demand for such rights. Classroom teachers had not been paid for over eight months. Lecturers had been demanding for improved pay package for a long time. Yet nobody listened to them. They complained about the poor funding of the university system despite the very large amount of resources that entered the national coffers monthly from oil revenue. Yet their research laboratories had become comfortable habitats for rats, cockroaches, spiders, wall-geckos and lizards. There was so much infrastructural decay which they could no longer bear.

Civil servants also complained of poor salaries that could barely feed them and their families. All that fell on deaf ears. The C-in-C was not ready to listen as he ran the affairs of the nation as he wanted it. He retorted that he asked for nobody's vote to become the C-in-C; so nobody should tell him what to do. He continued to do whatever he liked to do and was accountable to no one.

It was at the same period of the labour unionists' protest that news filtered into the ears of the masses about the inhuman treatments being meted to some captives of the regime—the captives of democracy who were clamped down behind bars in various prisons and cells in the country. Chijindu and Benjamin, for instance, were said to be given a gravel-mixed breakfast of jollof rice everyday and a scanty, meatless, watery, slippery ogbono soup and gari for dinner. Sometimes, it was said, they were chained in dark humid cells like condemned criminals. Access to visitors was a luxury which they were not given. And they had begun to grow so lean like HIV-infected patients. Chijindu's eyes were said to be looking like that of an ageing owl as a result of malnutrition. And all the cries and efforts of his wife to locate him and give him her food proved abortive.

Students of some tertiary institutions had also wanted to join their masters in protesting against poor academic environments, and against the astronomical increase of their school fees. But the

C-in-C's response was swift. He quickly ordered for a number of some Cobra Armoured Personnel Carriers mounted with powerful weapons to be stationed at the main gates of those institutions, with a company of experienced combatant soldiers to man them. That was the formula that nailed it. The students hurriedly ran back to their hostels to brood and grumble over their problems.

As the June 12 rally progressed from Allen Avenue, more and more people joined them until they became a mammoth crowd. On arriving at Ikeja Central Business District, Shola promptly mounted a platform to address the people as he was solidly flanked by Obeche by his right and Tope by his left. Shola thundered with all the strength he could muster:

"I am an incorrigible and unrepentant June 12 fundamentalist. I stand on June 12, with June 12 and by June 12! We fight on principles and will continue to fight on behalf of the people. I will die for the people of this country! This Rugami environment is that of Hitlerite dictatorship and Nebuchadnezeresque oppression. It is informed by corruption, nurtured in perfidy and conceived in debauchery. A nation that harbours the majority of its population in poverty offends God. Our governments harbour poverty and so they have offended God. This nation is too rich to be poor. There is too much congenital injustice, demonic oppression, ruthless dictatorship and agonizing poverty in this country today. Until these destructive vices of governance are uprooted from this country, continuous imprisonment or even threats of assassination will not deter us from the people's cause. We the masses..."

There were still words in his mouth when riot policemen began to shoot tear gas in all corners of the crowd. It was so suffocating that the people quickly dispersed in all directions. One of the men, Mr. Bunie, was rushing to cross a nearby busy road when a vehicle crushed him to instant death. His brain was littered on the high way while his blood spilled over and coloured the road, glistering with the scorching sun. Shola wept when he learnt of Mr. Bunie's painful death. Expectedly, he was apprehended. They hit him repeatedly with the butt of a gun; beat him ruthlessly before taking him to Force Criminal Investigation Department at Alagbon, Lagos where he was detained for several days before he was released with bloodshot eyes. That same day, Obeche and Tope got several threat calls. But they did not accept to succumb; did not agree to surrender.

One week after the rally, it was learnt that members of the C-in-C's strike force and killer squad were seriously on the heels of Obeche. They pursued him up to Ikeja Airport where he narrowly escaped death en route London where he stayed to continue with the protest against the murderous regime. Then they began to search for Tope again.

The C-in-C continued to direct the affairs of the nation with a finger of iron. He seemed to be drunk with the intoxicating wine of power which he wielded to the maximum. Dialogue and consultation on national issues were seen by him as a sign of weakness, and he did not want to be seen as a weak ruler. He was a maximum dictator. Then there was the love for diabolism. He began to fortify the throne with blood—the blood of the innocent; the blood of the oppressed. Witch doctors and occultists from different parts of the globe were regularly invited to the villa. They would, sometimes, prescribe human sacrifices in order to fortify the highly coveted throne. This was in addition to a multitude of cows that were occasionally buried alive for the same purpose. A story was once told of Rugami visiting the residence of a powerful marabout in a neighbouring country to inquire about who might succeed him so he could hunt down the person before any damage was done. "He is called a messenger of peace," the heavily bearded witch doctor was said to have blurted out. When he returned back to the country, he was said to have started tracing the name the way

Herod traced for the infant Christ when the three wise men from the East informed him of His birth in Bethlehem. He was reported to have found him, and then started plotting for a systematic elimination.

In a bid to hold on to power for life, he strengthened and intensified the activities of the strike force, his private killer-squad. The dangerous squad was commanded directly by the C-in-C and his chief security officer, Colonel Musa, a mosquito-voiced powerful officer. The C-in-C reasoned that he needed a secret rapid response squad he could command directly to deal more ruthlessly with the opposition which had increased geometrically against his rulership, just as the number of praise-singers around his table had also increased. The K-squad was made up of energetic and ruthless young men in their late twenties and early thirties, carefully selected from the police and the army. They became more dangerous than viper as they were given several trainings that stripped them of normal human feelings of sympathy. So their hearts became as strong as iron. They pursued their assigned preys with vigour and crushed a number of them without mercy. They were also ordered to mow down whoever stood on their way in discharging their assigned duties.

As these aggressive and remorseless tigers pursued and attacked the opposition, blood flowed ceaselessly on the land. Adetutu, Kunle's powerful wife fell for their guns. She was gunned down in the month of June while driving in the city of Lagos. Admiral Omote was also gunned down in his Lagos residence at night by "unknown" gunmen. Unknown gunmen! He bled and died in the pool of his own blood. The killer boys were usually rewarded with enormous cash and choice properties. So they were very willing to spare nothing in order to maintain their high material status. They showed unflinching loyalty to their Oga, obeying every order from him to the later: maiming, assassinating and chasing about some

147

noble citizens who belonged to the opposition. Those they were told not to eliminate out rightly, the police or army were ordered to arrest and chain like bandits in various prisons.

The C-in-C was in love with the game of power. Yet the game of power, sometimes, consumes its players. Even mere spectators could be inflicted with severe injuries. It could be a very dangerous game when it is played with crookedness, perversion and injustice. In the game of power, truth, transparency and altruism could be the unfortunate casualties. These noble virtues are murdered without mercy. Unbridled power intoxicates. It gave the C-in-C the prospect of endless glory as he sat comfortably on its chariot. Yet the chariot of power could carry its rider beyond the limits. When a rider perishes, the chariot beckons yet at another, with its characteristic allure. The chariot of power usually outlives its riders. It could be very deceptive. And when it is fuelled with sycophancy, it glows with pride and glory. That was the chariot the C-in-C rode with reckless abandon.

The high-wire military politics being played by him and the mafia that surrounded him began to engender fear and suspicion among the top military brass. A number of pepper-soup Generals struggled relentlessly to be in the C-in-C's good book; just to *chop*, just to ensure their safety. So the military began to turn into a carnivorous institution. There was a particular case of a Lagos military administrator who narrowly escaped bomb explosion said to have been planted for him by some of his allegedly jealous colleagues in uniform. No one was sure of safety anymore. Generals began to suspect one another and carefully chose and counted their words in discussions. No one knew who was a stooge. One could be roped up in a phantom coup if he was not careful. The brilliant careers of many officers were ruined through that way. So everyone counted his comment before making it lest he loose his head or career.

Chapter Fourteen

Shola was in his sitting room listening to the evening news when CNN announced a fresh sanction against the nation by the European Union on account of her rating by Transparency International as the most corrupt country under the sun and for arresting, torturing and detaining many innocent citizens who were opposed to military rule. The sanction was to the effect that no European investment would enter the country again, and that the C-in-C and members of his ruling council were forbidden from stepping into any part of their continent. When the news caster ended the announcement with the statement: "That traumatized African nation has been in the tight grip of iron-fisted dictators for too long a time, and really needs a breath of fresh air," Shola shut his eyes and wept bitterly in his heart. He wept until he forgot the dinner his senior wife had kept for him on the dining table; until the woman came and consoled him, and pleaded with him to eat his food so he would have the energy to think and plan as he was already doing. He obliged. Yet the dinner of yam porridge with chicken was so heavy in his mouth. He ate a little and dropped his spoon. Then he took a glass of red wine before he retired to his room with a troubled mind.

Shigaro was in the officers' mess at the 14 Battalion sipping a big bottle of Guinness Stout, after he cleared a plate of well prepared cow leg pepper-soup, when the news of the fresh sanction flashed on the television he had been watching. He sat up attentively from the sofa he had been relaxing, and glued his ears to the details until the news caster made the concluding statement which made him a bit uncomfortable. He had received with joy the news of the prohibition of the C-in-C and members of his ruling council from stepping into European soil, but the comment of a "traumatized African nation" being in the grip of "iron-fisted dictators for too long a time" was not good news to his ears. He saw in it a danger to his own ambition and dream. Would they slam the same sanctions against him and his council when he took over? Why were the Europeans bothering themselves much for what did not concern them? If Nigeria was ruled by soldiers, was it their business? Why would they always refer to soldiers as dictators when they were in positions of governmental powers? Anyway, had they really succeeded in short-changing the C-in-C since they started imposing their sanctions on him and the country? He concluded his thoughts on that note, finished his drink and proceeded to his house. When he got in and banged the door after him, he picked a biro and continued with his plot.

It was yet another tragic news to the nation when it was heard that Brigadier Sule had died in Abakaliki prison after he was given a lethal injection by one Dr. Death in khaki uniform, just a few days after the sanctions from the European Union. He was one of the numerous political detainees of the regime until the C-in-C decided to nail him once and for all. He had alleged that the retired General and his former boss, General Makinde, had participated in a secret plot to oust him from the seat of power. Mrs. Adetutu Kunle, Pa Bozimo Rene, Admiral Elegbe, Alhaja Suliat Deji, Mr. Bunie Eric and others had gone earlier; now Sule had followed suit. Nigeria wept.

There was anger and bitterness in the hearts of the progressive forces. There was also fear of the safety of other detainees. No one knew who was going to be the next target for lethal injection; who Dr. Death might visit next as he went for his ward round. They all seemed to be at the mercy of the C-in-C. Shola spoke in anger, as though his heart would explode, in the various press interviews hegranted. As if he felt that that was not enough, he went ahead to write an open letter to the C-in-C, which was widely published in various newspapers:

AN OPEN LETTER TO THE HEAD OF STATE: QUIT POWER FOR GOOD: NIGERIANS ARE SUFFOCATING

In view of the present state of chaos our dear nation has been plunged into

by your government, I deem it very necessary to remind you of the crucial need to quit the stage now. You are fully aware that the wave of democratic order and good governance is what is currently blowing all over the world. Nigeria cannot and should not be an exception.

It is on this premise, therefore, that I am writing to re-inform you that military dictatorship is no longer fashionable but rather crude, immodest and out-dated. So there is no other option than for you to return the country to constitutional and democratic order. There is so much poverty, suffering and killings in the land. We cannot afford to remain where we are presently because it is certainly not the pathway to progress and dignity for any nation. We are in dire need of a civilian elected democratic dispensation and good governance. No more retrogression; no more stagnation; no more anarchy and iron--sted dictatorship.

Our present economic situation is causing untold pains to the average citizen. Considering our numerous sanctions and isolations, it is obvious that we are turning

151

into a pariah state. This trend must not continue because it is ugly and dangerous. We cannot afford to continue to mortgage the future of our children and the destiny of our dear country. Nigeria is terribly suffocating under your rulership, and would need to breathe the fresh air of freedom lest she dies. There is no other alternative whatsoever.

Let it also be clear to you that history shall judge you and whatever your government is doing presently. Everyone shall be remembered either for good or for evil. But you would have chosen the path of honour if you quit the stage now and return the country to democratic, orderly and accountable governance.

Shola got the response for his audacity three days later when security operatives raided his chambers; ransacked and up-turned his documents and files so that the whole place was in a shambles. The guards on duty were beaten mercilessly and one of them was shot at his leg. But they did not find Shola in his chambers. That same evening, they proceeded to his Ikeja residence where they subjected members of his family to enormous emotional and mental torture.

Shola and his family were having a dinner of pounded yam with vegetable soup stuffed with both fish and meat when a combined team of soldiers and mobile policemen arrived. When they heard a station wagon screech to a halt at their gate, and the violent banging of its doors as its occupants speedily alighted from it, they certainly knew that some dangerous guests were around. But it was no longer new to them. The guests broke through the gate, handcuffed the guards on duty and proceeded to gain entrance to the main building. Shola perceived what was happening and simply ignored it and urged everyone at the dining table to continue with the dinner. Some did, some did not because their hearts were already gripped with fear and uncertainties. As soon as the heavily armed men arrived at the expansive dining, Shola welcomed them to their dinner. They were eight in number, including their driver who knew all the routes in Lagos at his fingertips, having grown up in the city before he joined the force; before he was selected for the killer squad.

"You are invited to our dinner," Shola said to them, as if they were normal visitors; as if they were earlier invited for a dinner party; as if he did not see their combat-ready kits—bullet-proofs gripping their chests, black brass helmets on their heads, solid combat boots, khaki uniforms and AK-47 assault rifles at the grip of their hands.

Their faces epitomized horror and the determination to cause harm; their teeth firmly clenched like those thirsty for blood. Yet Shola was not scared. He simply continued eating his food when they expectedly ignored his invitation. There was silence everywhere, except that the menacing stare of the visitors caused enormous commotion in the hearts of the women and children, especially the females. The huge leader of the team had been hitherto staring at both Shola and his wives, without a word yet. He shifted his reddened eyes from one person to another, then to another. But it was more on Shola who now did as if he did not notice their presence in the first place. The team leader angrily broke the looming silence by himself:

"You are the Shola who has been troubling this administration; who has chosen to be a thorn in the flesh of the government!" he roared like an insane lion, baring his teeth in undisguised anger.

"Mal-administration, you should say!" Shola thundered back, "and I have no apology whatsoever. Tell your pay master that the masses of this country are suffering and I cannot keep quiet. Tell him that people are dying; that he is suffocating us and I cannot hold my peace. Tell him that a tuber of yam now costs three hundred naira; that an average citizen cannot afford three meals per day, tell him that our educational system has terribly deteriorated under him; that some of our graduates cannot write good letters; that their teachers teach with empty stomachs; that our research laboratories have rusted, tell him that corruption and ineptitude have eaten deep into the fabrics of our country; that the poor masses live in perpetual fear under his regime; tell him to restore June 12 mandate which he brazenly stole from us; tell him that we did not elect him to lead us. In fact, he is morally unfit to be ruling this country..."

"Pick him up!" roared the team leader. The boys handcuffed his unwashed hands and began to drag him down the staircase. They pushed him into the boot of their wagon and drove off. His two wives simultaneously yelled out in pain; hot tears streaming down their cheeks. He was taken to Panti police station where he was tortured and ridiculously quizzed by the boys. They finally dumped him inside one of their dark, humid cells.

Shigaro read Shola's open letter to the C-in-C with so much delight. If for no other thing, it had further portrayed his rulership as unpopular and unwanted in the eyes of the people and, indeed, the entire world. But he certainly was not happy to read from the same letter that military style of government was no longer fashionable but rather "crude, immodest and outdated," and the urgent need to welcome the breeze of a democratic system. He also was not too comfortable that the letter said something about the judgment of history because he never liked the word 'judgment.' It usually gave him some unpleasant feelings.

When the news of Shola's arrest filtered into the ears of the masses whose advocate he was, it sent many mourning. He had been their symbol of hope and justice. In him they saw a lion-hearted activist, a willing patriot, a sacrificial leader, a compassionate ally, a tireless mentor, an incurable optimist and an irreplaceable democrat. There was fear in the hearts of many concerning his safety this time around, especially as they thought of the fact that the C-in- C had introduced another dimension of torture and extermination; lethal injection. Would he also go the way of Adetutu, Rene, Omote, Sule, Elegbe, Deji and others? Would he ever be released again? Would Dr. Death spare him this time? There was palpable fear. Some days later, posters and handbills began to spring up in various streets in Lagos. They were pasted on fences, school premises, coconut trees, mango trees, gmelina trees and gates of some residential buildings. They contained only three words printed in bold, dark capital letters: **FREE SHOLA NOW!** Again, the various prodemocracy groups began to put plans on the way to organize an engulfing protest which could have been the mother of it all. Four days later, Shola was released from Panti with bloodshot eyes and a swollen leg which the police had repeatedly hit the butt of their guns. He recovered on a hospital bed two days later to the joy of the masses.

News filtered into many ears that the C-in-C was not in good health condition. But many rather reasoned that he was having a sober reflection. Perhaps the turbulence, open letter and series of protests had begun to gain entrance into his ears. No doubt, he had trampled on many lives and inflicted severe injuries to many souls. He knew that his *sword* had made some women childless; some widows and some children fatherless. There was a great feeling of uncertainty in his mind. He reasoned that he might not be lucky to step aside into safety. Where was his hiding place? He could not imagine himself being humiliated after enjoying the good things of life in very high places. So he stuck to his gun; he maintained a tight grip on the trigger from where his authority emanated. He decided for better or for worse. By the way, who was more qualified than him to rule Nigeria?

As more pressure mounted on the regime, the C-in-C also intensified his despotic propensities. The security agencies and the strike force became more brutal to the opposition which had now resolutely vowed not to allow the regime a peaceful night sleep any longer. There were the angry labour unionists, the unyielding NADECO, the uncompromising CD, the irrepressible PRONACO, the determined CLO and the recalcitrant press. The C-in-C hated them with disdain and now ordered his strike force to hunt down the ring leaders of the groups. So they went after them with vexation. He maintained that since he did not ask for anyone's vote to come to power, no one should tell him what to do or when to leave.

The most hated sect among the opposition groups seemed to be the gentlemen of the press whom the C-in-C accused of constantly damaging the image of his "hard working regime" through the various "nonsense" they publish in their papers. So the strike force went after them with more indignation. They chased after them from their residences to the streets; and from newspaper stands to press buildings. They were ready to pay the supreme price for the freedom of their fatherland. Bugada Shittu had fallen earlier. But his colleagues who were still alive remained undaunted. The gentlemen of the press metamorphosed to the radical men of the press in their struggle to rescue a suffocating nation. They were more determined to fight the junta to a standstill even though they had only biro as their weapon. They vowed to stay in caves, if need be, to do their job; to fight for freedom from oppression.

Suddenly, the C-in-C announced a transition to civil rule program. But he meant it to be a dummy political agenda; a deliberate ploy to deceive the nation again. It was yet another political maradonism. He approved five political parties which later turned out to be the five ugly fingers of a leprous hand. When the announcement of the transition programme was initially made, many gullible citizens shouted "hurray!" But they did not know. They did not know that the C-in-C was only playing a game; a well calculated game of power. Then he began to push out more Ghana-must-go to his conscienceless pipers all over the country.

The dog said that it faithfully follows a man with a fat stomach for two main reasons: if he does not defecate, he will certainly vomit. So the pipers multiplied around him. They were prepared to tell him whatever he wanted to hear, provided they continued to get the crumbs of hot cake that fell from his dining table. Government radio and TV stations sang his praises at regular intervals while his paid pipers composed more new songs and supplied to them:

Rugami is a great son
He is a messiah and a hero
The mother that gave birth to him
Gave birth to millions
In just a single childbirth
Let it be well with him
Let him be blessed with
Good health and long life
So that he will continue
With all the marvellous works
He is doing for the nation
He is the saviour we need!

Whoever sees Rugami
Should embrace him and tell him
That we feel his good works
That we smell a pleasant flavour
That our country has been better
That our land has been sweet

Ever since he climbed the throne
So call him the good leader
Call him the great hero
That cares for the poor and the needy
Call him the sun that rises in the morning
Call him the moon that shines at night
Call him the star that brightens the firmament
Call him a thousand names
Yet they will not be enough
So we really thank him
He has done so well
No vacancy in the villa!

He enjoyed every bit of the eulogy; he had been caught up with the intoxicating dance of power. Yet there was fear in the hearts of some discerning citizens. No one knew precisely what the pregnant nation would deliver in the long run. To the C-in-C, it was a sweet and pleasurable dance. But to the masses that had borne the brunt of pains and sufferings for long, it was like an elephant trampling on a field of carpet grass. The elephant could feel the pleasure of the trampling game but the grass certainly suffers. He did not care; he did not want to know; he had the military in his palms. All the opposition groups put together now seemed to him like a single man throwing pebbles at a brick wall. He was like a man who took an overdose of marijuana. Whenever he looked at human beings in that state, they would appear to him like insignificant ants.

When the shattered remains of Mr. Bunie, the crushed activist, was brought to his country home for interment, tears flowed ceaselessly from the eyes of the people. His widowed young wife seemed inconsolable; likewise his three little children and aged mother. Their morning had turned into midnight; their tears flowed like a river.

One year after his demise, he was commemorated with a memorial lecture organized in his honour in Lagos by the organization he worked for. It was an unpublicized lecture because the organizers wanted to avoid the prying eyes and embarrassment of security operatives who were now on rampage for their master. In attendance were some top members of various pro-democracy groups who had not yet been chased out of the country or hounded into detention. Shola was the guest lecturer. He delivered a paper titled: **The Struggle for Democracy in Nigeria: No Turning Back.** As he spoke, and counted the gains and the pains, tears flowed freely from the eyes of many participants. Some held their breath and listened with rapt attention. The sacrifices and loses were really enormous while the gains so far seemed too little. Shola thundered from the podium, punctuating his speech with his index finger and stamped that there was no going back until victory was achieved. He urged Nigerians to sustain the struggle even if he himself died in the process. That would be a worthy sacrifice, he said:

> "...I did not determine the day I was born and cannot determine the day I will go... even in death, there may be triumph, even in living there may be loss and failure. Living in compromise is a disastrous life; particularly when what you are fighting for is fundamental... let me say it again so that Nigerians will know. It pays to fight for the cause of the poor, the needy, the persecuted, the neglected, and the cheated in the society. Mr. Bunie had paid the supreme price for his fatherland... I am not a middle–of–the–road man. What I believe in, I pursue intensely. I put my life on the line. I therefore challenge all well- meaning Nigerians to..."

When Mr. Bunie's widow was called upon to address the audience, hot tears raced down her cheeks as she gripped the microphone. But her words were clear and firm. She thanked all the participants for the posthumous honour they had come to bestow on her husband and also pledged her unflinching loyalty to the course of democracy. She went ahead to declare her intention to mobilise her fellow women to join in the fight against dictatorship. When she notified the audience that each of her three children had lost a term in school because she could no longer afford the bills alone, a female member of the audience sprang to her feet and told her not to cry or bother about that anymore; that she would foot the bills henceforth; that she had granted scholarship to all of Bunie's children up to the university level. And there was a deafening applause. Her name was Adelaja; a noble woman who traded in gold and jewelleries, and had seven sons and two daughters that deeply cared for her. The gathering ended with a solidarity song.

The music in the political arena began to change gradually. As the C-in-C began to change his dance steps, the paid pipers altered their rhythm and lyrics along. It was the self-transmutation proposal. Since the major pressure and demand of the people was for civil leadership to come on board first, he began to unfold some well-coded plans to remove his khaki and transmutate to a civilian president. It was a confusing mathematics to many Nigerians. In a matter of weeks, he had completely bought over the five political parties he had permitted to exist. Then they began to compose one common song: we have adopted Rugami as our unanimous candidate for presidency! Many could not take the song seriously at the initial stage. "No! Such a thing will never happen in Nigeria," they had said. Meanwhile many well-meaning citizens had been intimidated out of the race so that "Oga kpata kpata" could have his way. It was like a mere drama, but it was real. Then it became obvious that the nation was about to be dribbled again. It was a rude shock to many people when the big-wigs of the five parties appeared on TV screen to openly declare their support and adoption of the C-in-C as their consensus candidate. "How much were they paid?" many had asked. Paid to sell their fatherland? Paid to sell their future and that of their children? Paid to mortgage the lives of the citizens? Paid to be enslaved for how long? Paid for what? In fact, there were too many questions without answers.

Shola was in his sitting room watching TV when he saw the unfolding drama. He could not believe his eyes. When the C-in-C appeared on the same screen a little later to thank all the parties for the "enormous confidence" reposed in him to steer the ship of state, Shola was mad with anger. His entire body system quivered and he became restless. He shook his head in dismay and broke down in tears; tears of sympathy for a drowning nation. He turned off his TV, sat down quietly and closed his eyes in un-subdued anger.

"Back to the trenches," he said to himself, snapping his index fingers. Then he rose and entered his bedroom. That night, Shola murdered sleep. All that was in his mind was the thought of what to do to salvage a drowning nation. At day break, he hurriedly took his bath and dressed up in a jet black suit, a black spec and a black pair of shoes to match. He did not remember his breakfast. He proceeded to the Federal High Court to file a suit to stop the C-in-C from implementing what he called a crazy and ridiculous agenda. But he already knew what would be the outcome: the court would not stop the moving train; the train on a very high speed. No, the C-in-C would not listen to the law because it was not the law that brought him to power in the first place. It was the barrel of the gun. Another issue was if the trial judge would even have the courage to deliver the right verdict on the case; the verdict against a stone-hearted dictator. The judge could lose his head on account of such.

So it would take a very courageous, patriotic and sacrificial judge; a judge who was ready to die, if need be. Shola knew it. So he also thought of a Plan B.

Seven days later, after he filed the suit, Lagos began to boil again. It was a great eruption of disorder as a tumultuous crowd of activists trooped out to protest, displaying their placards, and chanting in anger: *Rugami must go! No self-transmutation!* When they converged at Broad Street, Shola stepped forward to address them. He wore a well-tailored white short-sleeve and trousers, with a white canvass to match. Shola's boldness and charisma radiated in the afternoon sun. His sudden emergence to address the people was like a ray of light appearing in darkness, and he was straight to the points.

"Great citizens of our fatherland," he began, his countenance now raw, grave and stony, and his eyes bespectacled with a sunshade. "We must not allow this sacrilege to occur, even if all of us would be sacrificed in the process. We must not allow democracy, equity and justice to be raped again in this country in the name of a transition- to-civil-rule programme. If a monkey wears trousers, it remains a monkey. If a baboon puts on a skirt it does not transform it into a marriageable lady. Even if a chimpanzee greets you 'Good morning,' it does not make it any less a chimpanzee. What makes a monkey a monkey is in its blood; likewise the baboon and the chimpanzee? In the same vein, if this man removes his Khaki to wear *agbada* as President, it does not make him any less a dictator. So we must not allow ourselves to be deceived or fooled. He is an unalloyed product of military tradition and command structure. There is nothing else he can change into. He remains a dictatorial soldier any time, any day, anywhere. So our struggle must continue. Great citizens of our land, will you allow this man to continue to impose himself on us?"

There was a thunderous and emphatic "No-o-o-o-o-!" which was stressed to the limits; to a breaking point. They sang the solidarity song, re-emphasizing that they would fight the course to the end; that they believed in, and stood for one united and prosperous nation; that they were ready to die for freedom from internal oppression and subjugation. The people dispersed for the day. The following day, news filtered into many ears that Shola's law chambers were riddled with bullets the previous evening, and that one of his guards on duty was terribly wounded. But they could not find him.

The C-in-C continued to sell his self-transmutation agenda to more disillusioned politicians who grabbed it with their two hands, and told him whatever he wanted to hear. *Man must wack, abi?* He made sure he increased the volume of Ghana-must-go bags of money given out regularly so that more and more people would be lulled and lured to join his bandwagon of paid pipers. It was money politics in action. When one of the paid pipers sold the idea of "One Million-Man March" to Abuja in support of the self-transmutation bid, the C-in-C purchased it without delay. Daniel Kunu was given a large volume of Ghana-must-go to mobilise one million hungry, impoverished, unemployed and frustrated youths to Abuja to declare their false support for Rugami-must-continue agenda. The boys were paid and brought from the creeks, jungles, deserts and hinterlands to behold the flashy city of Abuja for the first time. It was a very beautiful city springing up overnight with glamour; a city jostling to be the pride of a continent.

When the boys from the creeks returned home, there was great indignation in their hearts, in their land. How could Abuja turn into such a flashy city overnight when their own land and people were neglected for too long a time? Why weren't the previous calls by some of their leaders like Koolo, to look into their developmental and environmental problems sincerely and resolutely considered? How could such a pretty mega city evolve in a distant terrain, in a twinkling of an eye, when the goose that was laying the golden egg had remained in squalor and in wretchedness? Why were there no access roads to their communities when everywhere in Abuja was nylon tarred, with breathtaking street lights? Why was there no light, portable water and good hospitals in the same land that harbours the nation's wealth, especially in the rural areas? Why were there no good schools? Why was poverty crawling on the same land that flowed with abundant milk and honey? Why was their water and land marred by the activities of oil exploration, yet no one seemed to have taken their plight seriously? Why were their youths hungry and jobless when the wealth that flowed from their land was used to provide comfortable employments to the youths of other clans? Why were they subjected to sub-human standards of living in the creeks when nature had actually showered abundant blessings on them? On the whole, why was development farfetched from their land when the Abuja of yesterday had already attained the status of a reputable mega city? All these questions inundated the hearts of the youths of the creeks when they returned from the Abuja One- Million-Man March. They wanted to know; they demanded for answers to these burning questions of their hearts. Then they remembered again that one of their heroes in the past had seriously asked similar question in his lifetime but was equally ignored.

For several weeks, various youth groups in the region continued to meet, to express their views over the situation. The mother of all the meetings came to be at Kaiama. It was there that a crowd of aggrieved youths in the region gathered to decide for themselves. It was there that a declaration was made:

"We cease to recognise all undemocratic decrees that rob our people and communities of the right to ownership and control of our lives and resources which were enacted without our participation and consent. Agree to remain within Nigeria ... and that the best way for Nigeria is a federation of ethnic nationalities..."

The youths stated that their declaration was in line with the Basu Bill of Rights which also expressed the desire of the people to have control over the milk and honey flowing from their land. They decided to take the destiny of the region into their own hands; decided not to be ignored any longer. They vowed to match force with force until they were given adequate attention. It was a vow that would later shake Nigeria; a vow that would draw the attention of the whole world.

Barely one month after the Abuja One-Million-Man March, Shola organized a Two-Million-Man March of all pro-democracy activists and patriotic citizens of Nigeria at Enugu. At the end, three million people attended it from various parts of the country. Polo field could not contain the people who later trooped out to the various streets from Zik's Avenue to Ogui, New Heaven and other major streets in the city to pass their anti-dictatorship messages to the inhabitants of the city and to the rest of the world. It was like a big slap on the C-in-C's face because it portrayed clearly that those who wanted him to go were more than the paid pipers who wanted him to stay. Shigaro was overjoyed at that critical observation as he tightened up his plot day after day. The group now met almost on a regular basis at various locations.

Captain Kokoma became ill on account of excessive work pressure from two different and silently opposing fronts. He was the commander of the recce squadron that was newly deployed to be part of the joint military and police operation that combated border criminals along the Lake Chad basin and the Mambila plateau in the North East, as well as an indispensable member of Shigaro's group. In fact, he was not just a member but a member of the inner circle which comprised of himself, Captain Curu, Major Kekuru and Major Shigaro the chief architect. And by virtue of being in the inner circle, he must of necessity participate in every meeting. This was because the critical use of tanks on the D-day entirely depended on him and the officers under his command. He knew it. Again, on the other front, he was not just a commander—the type of commander who sat on an executive chair in an air-conditioned and well-furnished office to drink coffee or beer and pepper-soup while dishing out orders to his soldiers in the battle field, but a very practical commander who more often than not led his troops by himself when the battle became fierce. Kokoma, most of the times, drove the lead armoured tank and fought the marauders to a standstill. For that, he was greatly admired and respected by quite a number of officers and soldiers in that joint operation. So when he became ill for over two weeks and was off duty, it became a big blow on the two fronts. Shigaro and the rest of the officers were highly troubled due to the captain's inability to attend one of their meetings within that period. A number of thoughts and possibilities came to their minds. Was Captain Kokoma tactically bowing out of the plot? Had he spilled the beans? Would they be rounded up any moment? Why would Captain Kokoma betray them? Why must he be sick at this critical point? Who would roll out the tanks which they must, of necessity, use in the operation? Was that a signal that the plot they had already invested so much in would fail? Should they disband and escape from the country immediately? It was at the thought and mention of this last point in their meeting that Shigaro stood his ground and said a thousand times no! He maintained that even if the plot had leaked, he would escape to nowhere; that he would still be in his office doing his normal work or in the officers' mess drinking Guinness Stout while waiting for the soldiers that would be sent to arrest him; that, for him, escaping to any place for a plot he had hatched and nurtured to such a critical level was tantamount to behaving like a woman, and that he was not a woman and would never be. When they saw Shigaro's courage and bravery even at such a point, their common faith in the course was strengthened. So they decided to watch and wait.

When Major Kekuru notified the meeting that he reliably gathered that Captain Kokoma had been referred to the military hospital at Yaba, it was resolved that Shigaro should go there as soon as possible to find out the exact situation. The next morning, he left early to Lagos. It was there that he met a rapidly recuperating Captain Kokoma on the hospital bed. Kokoma welcomed him and asked him to sit down on a plastic chair closest to him; from where they could communicate without raising their voices. When Kokoma informed him that excessive regular stress was responsible for his sickness, Shigaro heaved a sigh of relief. Then he told him of the palpable fears in their last nocturnal meeting. But that was not before Kokoma mildly signalled the young female nursing officer that had been attending to him to give him a little time to speak with his visitor. On hearing of their fears, Kokoma smiled and then reassured him that they were still together; that he was not the type of person that could do such a thing; that he would never be a traitor in his life; that he would soon be back to their meetings. Shigaro was greatly invigorated. He bided him farewell, telling him to get well soon. Then he returned to base and convened another meeting within seventy-two hours. The officers gathered again and heard the good news that eliminated their fears.

It was nearly a month before Captain Kokoma resumed his command of the recce chaps in the North East amidst a rousing welcome. His troops rejoiced and threw a free for all party the same day to celebrate his return. Kokoma was elated and at the same time humbled to see such a reception in his honour. Shigaro and his group were equally excited to hear that Kokoma was back to health and to command. They were much happy when he personally rang a few of them to inform them that he had recovered from his ailments, and also reassured them of his commitment to their common course. They were all joyfully relieved.

On hearing that Kokoma was back to health and work, Shigaro scheduled a meeting of the inner circle again. This time, they met in his residence at 14 Battalion. This was the first meeting they had ever held in his residence. First, they celebrated Kokoma's recovery with chicken and champagne before returning to the grave matter at hand. Again, they reaffirmed their commitment to the course and requested Kokoma to report on the armoured tanks they believed they could secure through him; how they would secure them, and how they would be utilised on the D-day. He rose to the duty, and gave a graphical and convincing account of his calculations to the admiration of the rest of the officers. They shook hands with him and urged him to critically monitor and strengthen those efforts and calculations.

He returned to command the next morning to discover that the border criminals had come through the desert again to attack some border communities, and to dispossess those coming to markets in Nigeria, from Niger, Chad and Cameroun, of their valuables. Captain Kokoma was so furious that he decided that the marauders would be fished out and dealt with by all means. So when the task force commander, a lieutenant colonel, got approval from Defence Headquarters and consequently ordered for a full scale operation against the marauders the next day, Captain Kokoma went extra miles in carrying out his assigned duties, and was wounded in the process.

The border criminals on that day seemed to be more determined. Unlike other days when they fired a few shots and then vanished within a few minutes, they stood their ground and engaged the soldiers in a fierce fight for half an hour. It was at the middle of the fight that Kokoma alighted from the lead armoured tank and fell on his belly with an M16. Then he began to subdue the marauders with precision and accuracy. He pounded them until they began to flee in disarray. As he rose to pursue them alongside the armoured tanks, one of the fleeing marauders suddenly stood, targeted Kokoma and fired the last bullet in his rifle. It would have been very fatal. The bullet seriously grazed his left shoulder and tore his uniform to shreds on that part of his body. He fell down on his belly again to avoid receiving another blow. But the bleeding was profuse. On seeing that the marauders had completely vanished away, the soldiers halted their pursuit and immediately carried the wounded captain first to their base. After a first aid treatment, the bleeding still continued because a very important blood vessel had been affected. It was then that an urgent arrangement was made, and he was flown back to the military hospital.

When the conspirators heard of what had happened to Kokoma and that he was back to the military hospital at Yaba, they were all shaken, except, of course the headstrong Shigaro whose career philosophy had remained to yield to nothing. As the plotters met again, silence dominated the meeting. Some of them believed that what had been happening to their colleague of recent was clearly the unseen hand of fate trying to save their lives from the claws of death by delaying them from carrying out an operation that would fail. Yet no one was willing to voice it out that way so he would not be seen as a traitor. Moreover, they were all co-travellers in the same boat and would surely be treated equally by the C-in-C and his loyalists if anything leaked out from the plot, irrespective of whose mouth it came from. As silence loomed in the meeting, Shigaro sprang to his feet with agility, courage and overwhelming strength which baffled the rest of the officers. He spoke eloquently, concisely and coherently to justify their conspiracy and to stamp that it was bound to succeed. By the time he finished speaking and sat down, their strength returned and they began to discuss the reports presented by certain key officers assigned to monitor some specific issues and developments.

The meeting ended with the resolution to wait for at least two or three weeks before calling for another meeting, so that Kokoma could possibly recover and join them. Shigaro proceeded to the hospital to see him the next morning. He was received with smiles by the amiable captain. Shigaro was greatly invigorated by that reception before he shook hand with him and they began to discuss in low tones after the nursing officer that was attending to him had departed. Kokoma reassured that they were still together, and that he too had a strong conviction that the plot would certainly succeed. Shigaro returned to base feeling much better than he came. He was so glad when Kokoma phoned him the following week to tell him that he had left the hospital and was back in good health. Once more, Shigaro quickly convened a meeting of the inner circle so they could begin to tidy up.

Chapter Fifteen

"THIS MASQUERADE MUST STOP DANCING!"
"THIS MUSIC MUST STOP PLAYING!"
"THIS RAIN MUST STOP FALLING ON US!"
" NIGERIA MUST BE FREE!"
"RELEASE POLITICAL PRISONERS!"
"CHIJINDU IS A PRISONER OF CONSCIENCE!"
"SET KUNLE FREE!"
"WE WANT DEMOCRACY!"
"RUGAMI MUST NOT SUCCEED HIMSELF!"
"WE ARE TIRED OF THIS REGIME!"
"GOD PLEASE COME TO OUR RESCUE!"
"O LORD COME AND HELP US!"

The inscriptions on the placards were uncountable. It was a NADECO rally at Yaba. Numerous progressive forces had thronged the streets of Yaba, to protest against the regime and against the self- transmutation bid. It was a tumultuous, uncontrollable crowd of aggrieved citizens. Shola was there.

As they sang and chanted solidarity songs, eight army trucks, fully loaded with soldiers, and three Saladines began to approach the people from various directions. When they got a little closer to the crowd, the combat ready soldiers alighted and began to encircle the people, shooting both guns and teargas sporadically into the air.

Then the people knew that there was great danger. They reasoned that no one ever confronted a lion with bare hands. So they began to disperse and disappear until the soldiers found Shola who refused to move an inch. When they threatened to shoot him, he tore his dress and faced the gun; that the soldiers could shoot if they wanted. But they did not shoot. They rather resorted to hitting him at random with the butt of their guns while some used their bare hands to slap his face; others punched him. Then they arrested and took him away. That was how the protest of that day died down. Three days later, news filtered into some ears that Shola was cooling his heels at Ikoyi prison. Then the "FREE SHOLA NOW!" posters began to spring up in every nook and cranny of Lagos. One week later, he was released with blood-shot eyes and a swollen face.

Major Shigaro of the 14 battalion was, again, greatly inspired by the most recent uproar in Lagos—the NADECO rally at Yaba, because it had once again shaken the foundations of the nation. Though the people had dispersed when they were severely threatened by the soldiers, it was like the mother of all the rallies that had taken place before it due to the number of people in attendance. It seemed to be greater than the number recorded at Enugu at the last rally. Both BBC and CNN had carried the news of the earth quaking rally to different parts of the earth. It had further portrayed the C-in-C's regime to be highly dictatorial and illegal, and that the citizens of the country were terribly tired of it. That was the type of report that went to different corners of the globe. So it made the regime to be more unpopular. Shigaro saw hope in such a scenario.

By now, he had already started putting finishing touches to his plot. With the vast financial resources at his disposal, he had no hitches whatsoever in any plans that involved money. There was a very rich Lagos-based businessman and fish farmer who was fully prepared to foot the bills and was really doing so. Shigaro threaded more meticulously to ensure that nothing leaked from the plot. It was already a matter of either life or death. He knew it all. So far, he had succeeded in bringing a total of eleven professionally sound officers to the plot—six majors, three captains and two lieutenants. There were twelve of them in all.

Major Shigaro Genje was a naked-wire adventurist and a career soldier trained at the Nigerian Defence Academy. He was dark, sizeable and stiffer than a rock. An embodiment of courage and competence, Shigaro was always willing to stake both life and career to achieve a set goal. Aside personal ambitions, his grievances with the authorities also stemmed from the fact that he had been severally denied promotion despite his achievements and exposures in the military. Most of his juniors were now his equals in rank while some of them who had *longer legs* had even gone a rank or two ahead of him. He was quite energetic, athletic and highly respected, especially among the Infantr y Cor ps for his professional dispositions and capabilities. He liked to be perceived as being tough and unyielding. He loved fame and power and loathed to be associated with lack and inadequacy. He was involved in three marriages which produced two girls and a boy who was his unmistakable carbon copy. He was forty-three years of age.

Major E.D. Ibodige was slim and elastic. He was an erudite intelligence officer - cool, smart, amiable and likeable. He had served as ADC to two military administrators and had enormous penchant to smell out troubles and dissect difficult situations. He was often seen with a smiling face and had a retinue of friends within and outside the military. Ibodige's favourite sport was golf. He could also use his leisure time to ride on horses where they were available. He had fantastic equestrian skills. He was fond of children even though he had not yet married. His major problem was that of choice because he had a lot of women beckoning at him. Materially, he was comfortable having being close to the corridors of power for some time. He wholeheartedly supported and joined in the plot because he believed that there was the need for a change in the baton of administration of the country. He did not like the chaotic state of affairs in the nation and reasoned that it was high time the C-in-C left for good. Ibodige had enormous confidence in Shigaro's ability to unseat the C-in-C having closely worked with him for six months in Liberia before he came back for his staff college course. He admired the enormous courage and confidence Shigaro always radiated as they worked together.

Major A.A. Bintuwa was a fine artillery officer whose spoken English was often marred with a heavy tribal accent. Nevertheless, he was said to be action-oriented as opposed to his soft, unassuming and innocuous appearance. He was fair and handsome, with a pointed nose which usually swept some ladies off their feet. Bintuwa hailed from a royal lineage and usually carried himself with an aura of royalty and prestige. He was a man of his own mind and words. He was a young lieutenant at Ikeja Cantonment, and was at the comfort of his bed in April, 1990 when Major Orkar and his boys struck. Since he knew nothing about it, he glued himself to his bed until the chaotic situation was over. His support for the plot stemmed from his personal belief that the C-in-C had actually overstayed his welcome and needed to go so that the nation would be rescued from its state of chaos and confusion. He never fancied the self-transmutation bid and had clearly said so to some of his closest friends. The thirty year old major attended Command Secondary School, Jos, before he expressly proceeded to the premier military Academy where he bagged a degree in law.

Major R.S. Zombe was short and fleshy. He loved the bottle and usually spent lengthy periods of time in the officers' mess. He had a retinue of women of easy virtue at his disposal. He could finish his monthly salary in one week before plunging back into indebtedness at the mess. Then he would eat and drink on credit until his salary for another month was paid. Zombe was in love with his career and would trade it for no other. He became involved in the plot after Shigaro sounded him at the mess while they copiously drank Gulder with a well-prepared, steaming cow leg pepper-soup. His commitment to the course was based on his belief that no condition was permanent. He reasoned that since the C-in-C out-staged someone, someone should also out-stage him, having been there for some dark years. It was not hard for Shigaro to get him involved. Once he understood that the dice was cast before him, he immediately pitched his tent with Shigaro whom he had first met at Jaji when they attended a course together. He was thirty-two years of age.

Major F.I. Idumoje was a mean and confident intelligence officer whose career was smooth-sailing. He attended King's College, Lagos, before proceeding to the Academy. He also attended Pakistani Staff College, Quetta and returned with excellent results. Idumoje was highly cerebral and focused. He was never a man of average in anything he did and hardly settled for the better when the best was possible and achievable. Idumoje hated injustice and oppression. He was outspoken, an extrovert by nature. As a stickler to discipline, the bespectacled Idumoje loathed to see professionalism compromised. His commitment to the course was based on his solid conviction that the nation would benefit by the exit of the C-in-C from the seat of power. He was happy with his work and had his eyes fixed at the zenith of the career. He was thirty- one years old and single because he was still searching for an ideal woman that could fit into his mould, taste and status. Idumoje had a high taste in everything - from his choice of automobile to the clothes he wore. He owned a brand new Toyota RAV4, with tinted glasses, which he, more often than not, drove in style and with an aura of dignity.

Major W. N. Donki was charcoal dark, skinny and stiff like a ramrod. He usually wore a natural humble appearance. But he was always on the bottle. An above average gymnast, Donki was a high achiever in sports during his cadet days and shortly after his commissioning. He became Shigaro's good friend from Liberia where he fought side by side with him as peace keeping soldiers. While he admired Shigaro's bravery and undaunted courage, Shigaro cherished his humility and simplicity of heart. Donki had a natural dazzling while teeth which he inadvertently marred with assorted kolanuts which he ate like food. He married a virtuous wife and had a retinue of children which his monthly salary hardly sustained but for his wife's hardworking nature and skills. Donki was a signals officer and had once commanded a battalion in Liberia. He was also in the Middle East as a military observer for one and a half years before returning to the country to continue with his signals job. His age-stricken father was a railway worker for thirty- three years.

Major U. E. Kekuru was a vibrant and highly respected recce officer. He was in his penultimate year at the Nigerian Military School, Zaria when he heard of Shigaro's heroism and exploits as they were returning from operation Duka Duka. Though he had never met him before, Shigaro was like his role model, and he longed to set his eyes on him someday. He was so glad the day they coincidentally met at Jaji at a particular seminar. Now they were equals in the force. He was strong-willed and principled. But his strong will did not compare with that of Shigaro. Kekuru was a bookworm and usually spent lengthy hours in his office. He rarely spent more than an hour in the mess and was widely known to be frugal in financial and management issues. He hardly wasted anything entrusted to his care. Moderation was a policy to him. Major Kekuru spoke of lawless English slightly garnished with Western accent. But his palms were smeared with super glue mixed with Aradite. He, too, never expected much from other people. He was a man that had contentment in whatever was duly his. He was twenty-eight years of age and married to a twenty-nine year old economist from Ahmadu Bello University, Zaria. The marriage was blessed with a male child. Kekuru was so engrossed with his career that he hardly remembered that he had a home, his native home, which he usually traced to visit once in a lifetime. He bagged a B.A. degree in English Language from NDA.

Major G.V. Shanga attended the University of Benin where he studied Electrical/Electronics Engineering. When his age long hope of working in either Shell or Chevron was severally dashed, he bought a Direct Short Service form. Shanga had been a very competent engineer officer for several years. But he greatly loved what was in skirts and, therefore, had a large number of mistresses upon whom he lavished a lot of money. He savoured every pleasure each day could afford because he believed that human beings were mere tenants on earth. He reasoned that no man knew when he would pack out. So he lived daily like a stranger; a pilgrim on earth. The major considered the officers' mess one of the best places to be, especially when he settled down on a sofa, with a full plate of nkwobi or cow tail pepper-soup facing him, and a fair complexioned mistress sitting by his side and beaming a regular smile. Then he would feel on top of the whole world. He had a penchant for sizeable fair mistresses. He was thirty-five years of age and married to a difficult older woman who gave birth to a boy and a girl in an interval of four years.

Captain T. D. Kokoma was an ex-student of Federal Government College, Enugu. Two years after he completed secondary education, he proceeded to Kaduna for a regular course at the Academy. He was gentle, simple and homely. He had a beautiful, lovely and loving wife who produced five children in quick succession. Kokoma was an excellent swimmer and an above

177

average sprinter. His extremely gentle mien could be mistaken for weakness. But he was professionally sound and capable. He could be loyal, even unto death, in any course he believed in. He was the very first officer Shigaro muted the idea of the plot to. And since then, his loyalty and commitment to it had remained unshaken. On a general note, Kokoma was a level-headed career officer who initially fixed his eyes on retiring as a major-general, with full entitlements. He cherished animal husbandry, particularly fish farming. He was twenty-eight years old.

Captain M.M. Curu was Shigaro's 2IC at 14 Battalion. He was very tall and huge and had a noisy personality, which, sometimes, scared some lovers of gentility. He was never a man of dull moments. His voice was, by nature croaky, like that of an excited toad. It was such that he always struggled inwardly to bring down his voice during interpersonal conversations that required some elements of confidence. He was soldierly and had a good command of the English language. Curu was a heavy eater and also loved the stick, particularly Benson & Hedges. He had a certain attachment to his mother whose last child he was. He drank the milk of parental kindness so much that he almost became a spoilt child. His mother never knew that he enlisted in the military until the day he returned home with a green khaki uniform, a well polished black boot and single stars on his shoulders as a newly commissioned second lieutenant. Before then, he had lied to her that he was working in the defunct Kaduna textile industry. He feared that the woman might be sick unto death if she knew that her dearest son had joined the career of people she only knew to be violent killers and rapist; people who were trained only to kill and to destroy; people who had no business with peace but rather thrived in wars and chaos; people who yearned for societal disorder and chaotic situations so they could fight with guns and bombs. That was the old woman's perception of the military work. Curu knew it. So he ensured that the unlettered woman remained ignorant of his real engagement until he returned home for the first time with army uniform after his commissioning. Curu's passion for military service was unquenchable. He never gave thought to any other career because he believed that he was cut out for the khaki job. He sat for the Academy examination for two consecutive years. He did not give up until he passed it and was duly accepted. He was twenty-nine years of age and married. The marriage was blessed with a daughter.

While he was still a cadet officer, he went home once or twice in a year with a few wrappers to present to his ageing, loving mother in order to consolidate his lie that he was working in the textile firm. Then the woman would rejoice and make two or three dance steps in appreciation as she poured blessings of long life, good wife, good children and prosperity on him. But when she saw him with the uniform of people she never liked for anything, she almost slumped on the ground. She visibly shivered with her walking-stick as she walked out of their house to welcome him when she heard some neighbours calling his name outside and welcoming him home. Her shivering began when she sighted the one they were welcoming and it was her dearest son in full military regalia. She became speechless, sorrowful and disappointed, and never listened to Curu's relentless entreaties. Five days after he returned to his duty post, he heard that his mother had died in her sleep.

Her hatred for soldiers was not altogether baseless. She was living in Port Harcourt with her trader husband and two children when the Nigerian civil war broke out. Then they were unable to return to their native land which would have been safer for them because it was not part of the ravaged Biafran territory. And when they heard Gowon say that the "Biafran rebellion" would soon be quelled through, probably, a "simple police action" in a matter of days or a few weeks, they were encouraged to stay. Later on, they also heard Ojukwu announce that no power in Black Africa could defeat Biafra. Ojukwu's announcement changed their hope to despair. At a particular time, the Port Harcourt Biafran militia group vowed to defend the city with the last drop of their blood and insisted that nobody should vacate. A bloody civil war ensured and lingered hopelessly from days to weeks; from weeks to months; and from months to years. By late May 1968, the federal troops of the Marine Commando led by Colonel Adekunle, the famed Black Scorpion, broke Biafra's 52 Brigade's stubborn and brave resistance and captured the city of Port Harcourt after several weeks of failed attempts. That day was a terrible one for the Curus as the over-excited troops went wild in jubilation for their conquest and forged ahead to consolidate it.

The fear of the conquest of the entire Port Harcourt sent the Curu's hiding in their bedroom at Rumuola. There was no route of escape; no place to run. In the evening of that same day, three Hausa soldiers burst into the compound and made straight to the ramshackle building. Seeing that it was locked from inside, they certainly knew that some people were hiding there. Perhaps some Biafran soldiers who could not leave the city on time; perhaps Achuzia the Hannibal of Biafra could be there; perhaps Madiebo and Onwuatuegwu were taken unawares; perhaps Efffiong and his body guards were hemmed in; perhaps they could be the lucky soldiers that would capture Ojukwu alive. They would receive double pay. That would also mean the immediate end of the fratricidal war. One of the soldiers simply retreated backwards and then landed on the door with a kick of his right boot. It blew open. Then they instantly rushed inside with their guns cocked, ready for action. But they were disappointed when they rushed inside the bedroom and found a man, his two little sons and a plump beautiful wife squawking like frightened hens and saying, "We are not I- gbos...we are strangers here...but we are not I-gbos...Please, do not harm us." The man and his family were confused as they uttered those words and waited for anything to happen. For sure, they knew that something would happen; something unpalatable; something not in their favour. They prayed that it would not be too severe; that it would not cost them any life; that they would just give them some dirty slaps and leave them alone. But it was not to be so.

One of the soldiers - a tall, huge, black figure with conspicuous tribal marks, pointed an angry finger at the man and retorted, "You are Igbo, you supply broken bottles and pieces of iron and nails for Ogbunigwe landmines, and you are a Biafran man." He mispronounced Ogbunigwe as Agbunigwe, replacing the letter "O" with "A."

"We-we...we are not Ig-Ig-Igbos," the man stuttered and shivered.

But he did not sound very convincing to the soldiers due to his state of confusion. Then his wife also joined to plead to the red-eyed soldiers to spare their lives; that they were not Igbos; that they had never supplied broken bottles or pieces of iron or nails for Ogbunigwe; that they were only entrapped in the situation; that they had wanted to leave Biafra earlier but were prevented by the Port Harcourt militia; that they did not like secession. Her voice of plea was womanly smooth and lovely. She repeatedly mentioned their tribe and even went further to speak its language. But the language was not a familiar one to the soldiers who rather took it to be, perhaps, one of Igbo dialects. Then the tall, huge black one squeezed the trigger at her husband's left thigh, releasing two loud and shattering reports.

The man screamed like a baby, grabbing his thigh with both hands and muttering some curses to the soldiers in their native dialect, too sure that they could not understand what he was saying, having heard them speak deep Hausa to one another before he was shot. But they did not end it there. They dragged him and his two sons to their sitting room, leaving him in the pool of his own blood, and returned to the bedroom to ravage the plump, beautiful woman. They were not in a hurry as they took their turns on her with relish while she intermittently screamed until there was no more strength in her to do so. Satisfied, the soldiers abandoned the family in great pains and vanished. It was a Red Cross team that later came to their rescue that same day. They gave them some first aid treatments and evacuated them to their hospital which was not far from the house. Though man and wife later recovered from their injuries, the scars never healed in their hearts. The woman always felt very sad anywhere she saw a soldier while her husband never ceased to curse people in uniform until he died, ten years after the war. And he would place the same curse on anybody in his lineage that would choose to be part of them. The woman later discovered that she was pregnant. She was confused as to the paternity of the child; was it for her husband or the soldiers? Nevertheless, it was her

baby. The baby grew to be as tall as her husband but as black and huge as one of the soldiers that forced himself twice into her and spilled some seeds. But she was not too sure. Yet the baby became the apple of her eyes. She never conceived again after his birth. She loved him as she did her husband. The genuine love that brought them together as husband and wife still held them firmly until they were parted by death. The baby later became Captain M. M. Curu, a man whose love for military service was unwavering.

Captain N.B. Nujer was a courageous, lion-faced artillery officer known for his characteristic bluntness. He was thick and muscular, and had wrestling as a hobby. His ears were almost as long as a rabbit's. Nujer was infinitely energetic. He was not a man of many words. His intelligent quotient was not on the high side, but he could be resolute and determined. Nujer loved adventure, provided he believed it to be just and worthy. He had numerous dependants who often made his account to be in red before he could receive another month's salary. Though he liked to have a very good means of mobility as his own, he had not yet been able to save enough money to achieve the purpose. He was thirty years old and planning to get married to a nursing officer who was a rank below his.

Lieutenant S. S. Limoena had an attractive baby face but with the heart of an angry tiger. To a first time observer, he could be perceived as being conceited. But he was not. Nature had only sold him away in that light. While in motion, he would seem to suspend his head in mid air. He spoke very softly, with a voice as little as his stature, though he was not necessarily a runt. He usually wore a tiny pair of glasses as clear as crystal, which often made him to look, all the more, effeminate. Limoena had a brain with enormous capacity for details. His inclination to mathematics and figures endeared him to engineering. He intended to make a great mark in Computer and Electronics Engineering, even as a soldier. He was twenty-seven years of age and was yet to give a serious consideration to marriage.

But he had two mistresses that regularly ate a chunk of his monthly salary. He detested alcohol and hardly touched the stick.

Lieutenant D. J. Badar was an affable, promising infantry officer. He was intelligent, tall, chocolate, and had a manly gait. Always clean-shaven, neat and spectacular, Badar had the tall dream of becoming a first class army chief someday. He was known for his calmness and patience in discharging his duties. He hardly believed that impossibilities existed; rather he usually viewed virtually everything from the angle of possibility. He believed that wherever there was a will, then there must be a way. It was not so easy for Shigaro to get him involved in the plot because he was, by nature, the least gullible. Nevertheless, Shigaro perceived him as one that would be very useful for the plan. So he continued to explore diverse avenues of capturing his mind until he got it, and firmly too. Once he had a personal conviction of the need for the plot, he threw his weight behind it and never looked back. Badar knew the route to the armoury of his unit. So Shigaro reasoned that such a person would be a great asset to his team. He was twenty-eight years of age and married with two children.

These were the officers who directly participated in the series of nocturnal clandestine meetings held at different locations. They were to mobilize and coordinate on the D-day which Shigaro kept a top secret to himself alone. In the course of their meetings, certain inevitable names cropped up; names they considered too dangerous to ignore if the putsch must succeed. So some officers were specifically assigned to take care of them by starting to monitor their daily movements so that they would not pose a serious threat on the D-Day.

It was yet another shocking news to the nation when it was heard that Lieutenant Colonel Kayode Olu had died in detention. The news spread like harmattan fire. Olu was roped in a phantom coup when he returned from France where he had meritoriously served the nation for several years as a defence attaché. When he was hounded into prison for the alleged plot, Olu was said to be tortured and maltreated regularly like a common criminal. He could not bear the indignity for too long. He became sick but was not given access to medical care. The man died.

Shigaro was now constantly at alert, monitoring every situation in the country. Gradually, the day, the long awaited day drew nearer and nearer. They met again and again, and then for the last time before the expected day. But it was a stale night. The appointed hour, the H-hour, was now less than seventy-two hours. It was now time to clearly share duties and reaffirm their commitment to the course. Shigaro could see the faces of some of his brave comrades looking bleak while some appeared very disturbed, like that of sheep being led to the slaughter. Lt. Limoena, for instance, looked so disturbingly hopeless, like one who had come to the end of the road while Captain Kokoma appeared like one who had lost an only son and had no hope of giving birth to another. Shigaro felt it, but he did not betray his feelings. He saw his duty as the leader and went straight for it. He took the bull by the horn as he sprang to his feet and spoke boldly, citing several instances from Ghana to Cuba. He took them down the memory lane of history, reminding them that they were not the first people on earth to choose the course they had already chosen for themselves. He stated that Nigeria was worth the trouble; that right from time immemorial, several men had been taking the destinies of their nations into their hands and had been succeeding. Theirs, he said, would not be different. He also restated the reason for their planned action - that the C-in-C and the mafia that surrounded him had plunged the nation into the pit of poverty, deprivation and restlessness due to their inordinate ambition to rule Nigeria for life; that the nation had drifted dangerously to a state of confusion and, therefore, needed to be salvaged through such a courageous action and determination. He re-emphasised the need for change and firmly stamped that there was no backward route as far as the plan was concerned.

The following morning, around 7.30 a.m, Dr. Konja, Shigaro's younger brother, telephoned to inform him amidst sobs, that Eneza had peacefully passed on the previous night at eighty-five years old. She had, actually, been suffering from diabetes mellitus for several years. But for Konja's relentless care, she would have died much earlier. Her last words to Konja were that he should remain united with his brother and never forget to be of help to the needy. Shigaro told Konja to embalm her until they made arrangement for her funeral. He promised to phone him in a week's time. Having said that, he volunteered no more words; he did not want any other thing to affect his thinking. His head had already been filled with plans and counter plans which had hitherto become part of his daily dreams. The D-day was now at the door step. The grave hour was no longer far; the hour they had been waiting for. It was to be a crucial hour - the hour that could significantly alter the journey of a tottering nation; the hour of uncertainties. It was no longer far. Shigaro had begun to count down.

As soon as he finished talking with Konja, he hurriedly took his bath and drove to his office to answer some classified phone calls and to give some coded instructions to his comrades in various locations. Captain Kokoma was to bring a considerable armour support from his unit while Major Shanga of the Engineering Corps was to take care of telecommunication lines. Shigaro had begun to prepare his mind to put pen to paper to prepare the draft speech which was to be delivered by Major Bintuwa on behalf of his comrades-in-arms, before Shigaro would come up with his maiden broadcast at the breaking of the day.

When Shigaro returned from his office that day, he decided to write the draft speech. It was a one page address. In it, Major Bintuwa was to announce to the entire nation that the former regime was dead, and would suspend the constitution and abrogate all decrees. Then he would briefly state the reasons for their intervention, and solicit for the support of the armed forces and the nation at large. He would warn intending dissidents that they would be ruthlessly dealt with. Furthermore, he would assure all foreigners of their safety and state the willingness of the new regime to respect all treaties and agreements the nation had with other countries or bodies. He would also announce the closure of all the airports, seaports and borders with immediate effect, until further notice. Then he would impose a dusk-to-dawn curfew and inform the people to await further announcements. It was not intended to be a long speech.

His maiden broadcast also contained similar messages, except that he took more time to elaborate on the various reasons why they decided to intervene, vilified the C-in-C's regime and stamped the determination of his 'Revolutionary Council' to bring definite positive changes to the country, without promising instant miracles as 'good soldiers.'

Shigaro inserted both speeches into a file when he finished writing them. Then he went to bed because he had become very tired. He had not really slept well for the past seven days or so, due to his numerous commitments. He woke up the following morning to hear that Generals Yadi, Abisa, Olan and other soldiers and civilians, including Major Dipe were arrested for allegedly plotting to overthrow the C-in-C's regime. Then he immediately began to make contacts, using coded words to inform his comrades to completely lie low since the security situation was bound to be too tight for their movements. They did.

It was so pathetic to see the arrested *powerful* generals and others melting under the lashes of Colonel Musa's koboko, body-tearing horsewhips and even his dirty slaps. The C-in-C's CSO showed them no mercy and treated them as harsh as he could. Then they were whisked to Lokoja to face a constituted Special Military Tribunal. It was yet another shock to the already suffocating nation. While a few people agreed that they truly plotted, many believed that it was all a conspiracy.

When the proceedings went on for a while, it was glaring to every discerning mind that the alleged plotters would pay the supreme price, especially the 'powerful ones' among them. It was obvious that the C-in-C would settle for nothing less than that. Only the hand of providence could deliver them from his powerful claws. The nation waited impatiently to hear the verdict of the tribunal. Again, it was so pathetic to see the arrested *powerful* generals melt under the intense heat of interrogation and fear of death. They knew it all; that it was either death or life. But death was nearer to them than life. Life seemed too far away at the moment.

Then the greatest shock came; a jubilant shock to many in Lagos, Port Harcourt and several other places; the shock of all shocks. No one expected it; no one foresaw it. Rugami had died; the C-in-C had suddenly kicked the bucket. The nation received the news of his death with shock and disbelief. How could the flesh-eating tiger go like that; just like that? Many did not believe it initially. But it was real. The man had died. Some said that he died after taking an overdose of Viagra and had performed incredibly atop a prostitute; some maintained that he died of heart failure; yet others insisted that it was the handiwork of providence to rescue Nigeria from his claws. There were different versions of the same story. Nevertheless, his death was to mark a new beginning for the nation. It turned a fresh page for Nigeria to, perhaps, begin with a legible handwriting; the handwriting the world could read and understand; the handwriting of governance that should lend voice to the voiceless—the handwriting of true democracy, equity and justice. Barely two weeks after Rugami's death, Major Shigaro received a signal to proceed immediately to the South Korean School of Infantry for a special infantry course while Captain Kokoma was directed to move to America for an advanced armour course. Lieutenants Limoena and Badar were sent to India and Kent respectively to pursue various courses. Captain Curu was posted to 82 Division while Major Ibodije was posted to 34 Battalion. It was nothing but routine military programmes and postings. Nevertheless, it suspended all the plans and actions that were meticulously calculated by the group; because a number of the key planners were now far away from one another. Moreover, the man they had been scheming to oust had gone and a new dawn had come.

When the new helmsman, an officer and a true gentleman, appeared on the screen and addressed the nation, he sounded very calm, unassuming and genuine. Some said that he was really sincere; others took his words with a pinch of salt. They said that they did not believe him because he was an integral part of the old system that had tormented Nigeria for a long time. But he said he would be brief; that he would not torment Nigeria like some others before him; that he would not sit too tight on the throne; that he would certainly return the nation to an orderly rule.

The people rejoiced and applauded the new helmsman, whose name meant "a messenger of peace," when he released political detainees, including the recently alleged coup plotters who had hitherto mingled with death. It was like the right step in the right direction for the new helmsman and for the bewildered nation. But Kunle was not released; and the nation was not told why he remained in detention. Some weeks later, the nation woke up to receive more shocking news; Kunle had died in prison. Some said he was served a "special tea"; others maintained that it was Mr. Death, the killer of every mortal that decided to take him. It was a great pain to the nation to hear that Kunle had died. He died with all his dreams for Nigeria as stated in his manifesto. He died with his dream of a better and flourishing country; where good food would have been put on the table for the poor and the rich. He died with his dream of providing portable water and uninterrupted power supply to the masses. He died with his dream of breaking the jinx of unemployment and destroying the yoke of poverty and hardship from the neck of the people.

He died with his dream of giving free education as a gift to all those who had hitherto no access to it due to the debilitating, crippling poverty level in several quarters. He died with his dream

189

of hoisting the flag of Nigeria solidly in the international scene, so that she could play an effective positive role among the comity of nations on earth. He died with his dream of making justice available to all. He died. He died. The man died. Tears flowed like the waters of the River Niger from several eyes.

Kunle's death sparked off another round of sharp, turbulent protest in Lagos, the city where his unlimited philanthropic gestures had changed many lives. It was yet another time to raise placards with countless inscriptions:

"WE SAY NO!" "WE NO GREE!" "WE NO GO GREE!"
"WHAT HAPPENED TO KUNLE?!"
"NIGERIANS DEMAND FOR EXPLANATIONS!"
"WE WANT TO KNOW!"
"IT CANNOT HAPPEN LIKE THAT!"

There were many more. The entire city of Lagos went agog in protest as soon as the news of his death filtered into the ears of the people. Old tyres were set ablaze at the middle of some highways while logs of woods were used to mount emergency road blocks on others. Some closed up their business premises, Danfo drivers and Okada men rode in frenzied manners to demonstrate their indignation. Some street roads were blocked with old tables market women used to display their oranges, pears, pawpaw, groundnut, guava in streets. It was a day of furry. Broad Street could not contain the crowd of people that gathered therein to demonstrate their anger and displeasure with the sad news. Shola was there. Amidst the tears of the people, he stepped forward on an elevated ground to address them. His face was equally heavy and gloomy, with a pair of dark spectacles covering his eyes. After he stood calmly for a little while for the angry crowd to be calm enough to hear his voice, he thundered out in his usual charismatic, heart-moving manner:

"Great citizens of our nation, I stand here today to say that Kunle has paid a great price for democracy in his fatherland."

He paused to survey the sea of heads and eyes fixed on him, and discovered that tears flowed from many eyes. He continued:

"The most significant way to honour him is to keep the struggle alive. Keep it alive! Keep it alive! We must not relent or compromise an inch until victory comes; until democracy and good governance prevails in our country. We must labour to bring freedom to our children and must not be afraid of the sacrifices involved. It is a worthy course. As I look at some diverse ugly occurrences in our continent, I weep for Africa. Think of Rwanda, Somalia, Burundi, Angola, Liberia, Sudan, Ivory Coast and other places where tyranny, tribalism, greed, selfishness and unbridled lust for naked power have made people to turn to refugees in their God-given lands. So the tears you see me shed here today are not only for the death of Chief Kunle. It is also for thousands of African children, teenagers, youths, men and women who are hungry, homeless, disillusioned and have no peace in their lands."

Shola paused again to breathe some fresh air. He was being choked with a multitude of words which ran out of his mouth in quick succession, as if each word struggled to come out first. Then he brought out a dazzling white handkerchief and wiped his sweat and tear-covered face. He continued:

"What have we done? Our problem is man-made because nature has endowed us with all it takes to be great. There is no reason why anybody should be poor in this country. The society is decadent. No good roads, no good railway, no appreciable waterway system. The health sector is dangerously non-existent. There are no good facilities for reliable diagnosis. Can you tell me that five thousand five hundred naira is a living wage? That is One hundred and eighty-three naira per day when one tuber of yam is three hundred naira. So, does that not mean offending the constitution? Every constitution has always been imposed on us. The British imposed, our own people imposed, the military imposed. There has never been one instance the people voted in a referendum or plebiscite on their constitution in this country. What we have in Nigeria today is a replica of the Stone Age barbarism in Britain in the sixteenth century. The emphasis has been on religion, ethnicity and downright capitalism.

"Yes, I am proud to be a confrontationist. I will stop being a confrontationist when we have a core of leaders who genuinely and sincerely serve the nation and are not served by the nation. Respect is borne out of trait of character. You don't need to be told when you see a good leader. You cannot but notice his good marks. We have all it takes to build a prosperous nation, yet our people remain at the mercy of poverty. Again, part of our problem is that there are some people who believe that they are born to rule while others are born to serve. That is wrong. But I see hope." He paused again, then added, "I see hope."

Then the voices of the people rose to the peak as they began to shout: "Hope for Nigeria! Hope for Africa!" He paused calmly to allow them give vent to their feelings. After a while, he continued again:

"Yes, I see light at the end of the tunnel. I see the light of democracy illuminating every dark and despotic corner in Africa. I also see the same light shining brightly in other parts of the world where tyranny is still prevalent. I see equity and justice flowing like rivers of living water. I see tribalism, nepotism and avarice being stamped out of the face of our national leadership. I see the very end of coups and counter coups in Africa. I see bribery and corruption being buried in a deep grave. That is my dream. There comes a time when the gun will be useless in the face of the mass of the people and I think we are fast approaching that day."

He ended on that prophetic note which marked the end of the riots and protests that day. The people brought down their placards and began to disperse in a mournful fashion.

The sun of democracy rose in the month of May, with great hope in its wings, when the new helmsman kept his word and honourably relinquished the reins of power for a democratic dispensation. Then the painstaking journey to nationhood began. It was like a man learning to use his right hand in his old age, after he was already used to his left hand. Hope rose and fell. Then it rose. It was like a journey on a road with multiple potholes and gallops. The drivers also did not find it funny because it was tasking; the journey of writing the wrongs of many years.

Nigeria's dirty linens were brought before Justice Puto, the laundry man, for washing. They were too dirty; too smelly. Did he really dry-clean them? But Mr. Justice was not given the power to do justice in the numerous matters of injustices brought before him. Shola was there; Bola Oluwas's mother was there. The pain of the untimely murder of her promising son was still strongly registered on her wrinkled face as she leaned on her walking-stick, moving at a snail' speed to testify before Puto panel. And considering the agony that solidly registered on her aged countenance as she sat before the panel, it was obvious that she might not leave the world a happy woman. The pain she had suffered for several years for the gruesome murder of her son might still accompany her to the grave. Perhaps she might get the long-awaited justice at the panel in Sheol. Perhaps the killer of her dear son, whoever he might be, could be there and then be remorseful to confess. Perhaps he could accept to appear before the panel in Sheol—where there would be no one above the law, no Big Fish, no Big Man, no Sacred Cow, no bribery and corruption, no more assassination, no "Nigerian factor" and all that.

The vehicle of democracy trudged on with hope constantly rising and falling. But the journey continued. Then there was a great turbulence in the creeks. It rumbled and rumbled and rumbled and shook the very foundation of the nation. The boys who went to Abuja for One-Million-Man march stirred others and made good the decision they took at Kaiama, the country home of one of their heroes past. It was a great uprising as the boys began to march force with federal force, insisting that the region should be looked after; that the goose that has been laying the golden eggs should not be left in perpetual squalor. When their voice was heard and responded to, peace gradually began to return again to the area.

The noble soul of Nigeria is in eager expectation of the long awaited hope; the long awaited change. The tottering giant is earnestly longing for renewal; starting from the hearts of the citizenry. Then there'll be true unity in diversity. National interests will become paramount. Tears will then truly dry up from the eyes of the people as a new, totally rebranded nation will emerge from the old rubbles. It'll be a truly democratic and transparent nation. It'll be a nation of peace, prosperity and probity which is needed everywhere in Africa and the entire world.

Author's note

It was a titanic battle by soldiers to control the wealth of the nation at the expense of good governance and the wish of the people. No doubt, the price paid for the present democratic experiment in the country is too enormous and demanding to allow a repetition for any reason whatsoever. *Shackles of Freedom* is a reflection of the high-handed dictatorship that obtained in Nigeria and other parts of the continent before the light of democracy gradually and faintly began to shine. It is unequivocal to say that diverse nations in the continent are measurelessly blessed with all it takes to thrive; all the potentials for greatness and excellence. But we have a common problem—a plague: we are unfortunate victims of leadership. In various countries of the continent, it is not uncommon to see a determined mafia in a power play; holding their nations to ransom; clipping their wings to their utter detriment. In the face of all these, where lies the hope?

The military as an institution with a defined traditional role of defending the nation from both internal and external aggression is a noble and highly respected one. But its relentless adventure into the terrain of politics in different nations of Africa over the decades has not helped matters at all. What we rather see is stagnation, retrogression and more crises, which are not usually settled with dialogue and consultations, but rather with the approaches of guns and grenades. Such settlements do not usually last long before it generates more crises. From Field Marshall Idi Amin of Uganda to Master Sergeant Samuel Doe of Liberia, then to General Sani

Abacha of the Nigerian Army, the story is the same, and the lessons are so glaring that unconstitutional takeover of any legitimate government for any reason whatsoever is dangerous. It only leads to a perennial management of avoidable crisis and a continual subjugation of the lives and rights of the people whose natural cravings are freedom, prosperity and peace.

There is also a great lesson for our capitalist political leaders who come to leadership with the mindset of building financial empires for themselves and for their children yet unborn, rather than seeing governance as a sacred trust that should be discharged with dedication, diligence, devotion and decency.

This book is not intended to whip up emotions or to be a reminder of our sad, painful past, far from it. It is rather a work of fiction. No doubt, mention has been made of certain key suspects and leaders within the historical context of the time. However, the characters, incidents, places and conversations are mainly the products of the author's imagination. The uses of names of actual persons, living or dead, as well as certain statements are incidental to the purposes of the plot. In a fiction of this model, a patriotic author uses his God-given pen to contribute in building a greater, better and an egalitarian society; where justice and peace flow like rivers of living water; a society where integrity and forthrightness are valuable virtues; a nation that is free from the captivity of corruption, avarice and tribalism; a stable, free, united and Godly society. But that does not rule out the realities of history. The life and times of the C-in-C, Shigaro and others should remain a veritable lesson to those entrusted with the sacred duty of governance both now and in posterity for power belongs to God. Those who spill blood in order to acquire political power or retain their positions should know that the blood of the innocent certainly speaks; that its voice cannot be silenced from generation to generation; that the wicked does not die in peace even though he lives for a thousand years; and that a day of accountability shall come. Our nations in Africa are tired of the politics of blood; politics of kill and take; politics of mediocrity. Now is the time to embrace the politics of decency and merit. I strongly believe that the time has come for Nigeria as a nation and a key political player in the continent of Africa to embrace clean politics.

It is worthy of note that between the period of a woman's labour and the consequent delivery of her baby lies the invaluable contributions of nurses and midwives. This is to say that this work would not have been done without the qualitative nurturing of many whose intellectual and moral property moulded me right from the cradle. I am referring to my parents and teachers at various levels. Various volumes of *TheNews*, *TELL* and *Newswatch* magazines were very helpful in my research. I am thankful to their publishers.

I am eternally grateful to my priceless father, Mr. Andrew Igwedimma Ike who reluctantly departed before sunrise. Dad, it was through your actions and words that it became engraved in my young mind that integrity and forthrightness are worthy virtues. *Ezigbo Nnem*, Mrs. Christiana Nweke Ike is a woman of virtue and valour. Mama, you are very important to me. Thanks immensely for being there for us. I doff my cap for you for being the veritable vehicle with which I was conveyed to the world as a citizen of the African continent.

Furthermore, I am measurelessly indebted to Miss Martha Ude who breastfed me academically many years ago when I sat to learn under her in the kindergarten school. As an enthusiastic academic up-start, I drew a lot of succour from Martha's motherly tutelage. I would gladly say that my pilgrimage in this sphere of human endeavour began under "Aunty Martha" as she was fondly called.

My inestimable appreciation also goes to my precious wife, Grace, to my elder brother, Chidiebere, to Rachael, my dearest elder sister, to my indomitable editor, Dr. O. M. Kwokwo and to Prof. Tanure Ojaide for his fatherly mentorship. Daniel Nwachukwu is an in-law as a brother. His type is rare. Mathias Ike, Alex Mba, Ifeanyi Ike, Veronica Ike, Obinna Ike, Uchenna Ike, Chikodi Ike, Patience Ike, Osita Ike, Tochukwu Ike, Chiamaka Nwachukwu, Onyeka Nwachukwu, Nonso Nwachukwu, Ebube Nwachukwu, Godwin Ejimori, Jane Ohagwu, Emmanuel Ude, Emmanuel Ibe, Robinson and Elizabeth Chukwunenye, Nwose Chibueze, Uchechi Okereke, Uche Ogah, Chinedu Ugwono, Richard Okafor, Chika Obasi, A.D. Focados, Ikechukwu Okorie, Iwuji Samuel, Christian Okafor, Sithole Musa are relatives, siblings, elders and friends more precious than gold. God bless Rev. J.B. Michael for that uncommon large heart that made a great difference.

May I, at this point, most profoundly pay my glowing tribute to my dynamic Headmaster at Central School, Uhueze Mr. Raymond Ugwueke for always believing in me. Mrs. I. A. Moses is a mother of many mothers. She deserves a big "thank you" for her words of wisdom and encouragement. Engr. Dika Alfred Moses is a rare Jewel of a father. No adjective in the whole world will ever be enough to qualify him. God bless you all. God bless Nigeria. God bless Africa. God bless his entire creation.

Printed in the United States
By Bookmasters